LOVE AT SILVER SPUR

LOVE AT
SILVER SPUR

•

MARDI PARRISH

AVALON BOOKS
THOMAS BOUREGY AND COMPANY, INC.
401 LAFAYETTE STREET
NEW YORK, NEW YORK 10003

96-1015

PRINTED IN THE UNITED STATES OF AMERICA
ON ACID-FREE PAPER
BY HADDON CRAFTSMEN, SCRANTON, PENNSYLVANIA

To my loving husband, Michael
for his unwavering support,
and to our cherished son, Alex, who constantly shows us
life is a perpetual force to be met with delight
and conquered anew each day.

Chapter One

"You think you should be waiting out here in this heat?"

Kaleene sprang from her perch on the drugstore windowsill. The woman who had been surreptitiously watching her through the glass for the last few minutes now stood in the doorway a few feet away.

"Folks that aren't used to this Texas heat? Well..." She paused and surveyed Kaleene's long sleeves and heavy skirt. "It can sneak up on them. You're welcome to wait inside."

"Thank you, but my ride will be here any minute," Kaleene assured her, trying to put on a pleasant expression as she spoke.

The jangle of a telephone flowed out the open door, along with a tendril of cool air. Kaleene leaned forward and felt the air brush across her moist brow.

1

The woman flashed her a broad smile, then disappeared back inside.

Kaleene slumped back into the thin line of shade afforded by the drugstore awning. How could she have gotten herself in such a mess? She surveyed the small cluster of stores and offices that made up the business district of Tumbleweed, Texas.

Since the Greyhound bus dropped her off here thirty minutes ago, two cars, three pickup trucks, and a jeep had passed this spot. Not a single one of them stopped at the drugstore.

Where was the man who was supposed to pick her up? He should have been here by now. She pulled her two well-worn suitcases back farther into the shade. Maybe she should go inside and call Dr. Corbin. He said in his letter that the local farrier would be at the bus stop to give her a ride to the bed-and-breakfast.

Shielding her eyes against the high noon sun, Kaleene leaned out and glanced impatiently up and down the brick street. Nothing in sight was moving. A few cars sat in front of the sandwich shop across the street. Most of the small, main-street stores and offices seemed deserted at this time of day.

This was no way to start a career. Kaleene shook her head at her own foolishness. Why had she, the top graduate of her class in veterinary medicine at Purdue, chosen to start her career in Tumbleweed of all places?

The dean had been so stunned when she told him of her decision to turn down a lucrative teaching position. He knew how well she could have used the money. But she had decided to take on a modest partnership, working with an elderly veterinarian in a small town in the panhandle of Texas.

"And this is where that decision has gotten me." She shook her head. "I'm baking to death, and waiting for a ride from a fellow who's probably in the middle of shoeing a horse right now."

The doctor would probably never realize she had arrived. She wasn't scheduled to begin work for another week. But Kaleene had plans for the few free days she would have here in Tumbleweed. Important plans.

First, drop off her suitcase at the inn. Then, locate the county courthouse. It shouldn't take long to dig up the records she hoped were there. After that? Her course was as yet unplotted.

Fretfully, she pushed back a strand of her honey-colored curls that had escaped the clasp at the nape of her neck. For a moment she contemplated searching through a suitcase for a rubber band. Maybe it would seem cooler if her hair was off her neck.

As she smoothed some of the wrinkles from her corduroy skirt a loud chugging noise reverberated up and down the still street. An antique Model-T Ford truck rattled its way down the rough brick street. It ground to a slow stop at the curb in front of her. The engine coughed a last gasp, and a bang vibrated the window behind her.

Finally! This must be Dr. Corbin's friend. Kaleene squinted through the glare the sun made on the flat windshield. As the driver got out, her eyes began to water, but she managed to make out a tall form in a black Stetson hat. The man seemed in no hurry to reach her. His steps were almost languid. Considering the heat that beat down on that black hat, Kaleene was amazed that he didn't run to the nearest scrap of shade.

"Well . . ." His deep voice drawled as his penetrating gaze roved appraisingly over her slim figure. "What's a—"

"This is all the luggage I have," she interrupted briskly, indicating the two suitcases at her feet. "I'm in a hurry to get to the Smiths' bed-and-breakfast. If you don't mind?" she added, arching her brows. Maybe that would get him moving faster.

The tall man's rolling gait carried him smoothly under the small slice of shade. He stopped close, very close at her side, and removed his hat. With a broad hand, he swept back a thatch of jet black hair.

Finally, she could get a look at his eyes. Piercing blue orbs, hooded with full, dark brows glinted back at her. He was clean-shaven, but his strong, cleft chin showed a darkening of whiskers that would quickly turn into a substantial beard if he skipped shaving for any length of time.

With an unconscious gulp for air, Kaleene righted herself and moved nervously away from the masculine presence she found so unsettling. She picked up her scuffed suitcases and stepped quickly through the hot sunshine to the rear of the shiny black truck. No footsteps followed her. She hesitated a moment, not sure what to do.

She turned back to the stranger. Standing in the heat, exhausted from the long bus ride, Kaleene regarded him. She thought briefly that she should be very irritated with him. But looking at his whipcord-lean frame, the casual way he rocked back on the heels of his cowboy boots, she couldn't bring herself to do anything but stare.

"The Bed-and-Breakfast Inn?" His tone sounded even deeper out here in the dazzling sunlight.

"Um . . . yes." She had to replace the pair of sunglasses she'd lost on the bus ride, and soon. "The Smiths' Inn. You do know where that is, don't you?"

"Well, I suppose I do. This town isn't that big, little lady." He arched his brows and finished with a wide grin.

Kaleene gaped at his even, white teeth. Was he making a joke of her question? If so, that smile was the most marvelous ending to a joke she had ever seen.

"Let me get those for you," he said as he put the black hat on again. With a casual stride he reached her and effortlessly pulled the suitcases from her slim hands.

Up close, his smile was dazzling, revealing dimples that formed brackets around his wide mouth. In her brown loafers, at a little over five and a half feet tall, Kaleene considered herself average in height. This man, who seemed so large, was no more than half a head taller than her. Staring at his parted lips, she realized that the small height difference brought his mouth very close to hers. She would only need to tilt her head back just a little . . .

He leaned around her and deposited the suitcases in the clean bed of the truck, his face mere inches from hers. Then he gracefully stepped back and opened the passenger door.

"This is very nice of you," she managed to murmur weakly as she moved past his lanky frame, her eyes raking over his broad shoulders. "I meant to thank you earlier, but I . . . You must be a very good friend of Dr. Corbin's to do a favor for him like this."

"A favor?" His compelling smile became tinged with puzzlement.

"Giving me a ride," she said while sliding in the cab. "I mean, you must know him very well. A farrier and a vet do work together on occasion. I suppose that's how you met? Shoeing a horse he was treating?"

"Logan! Logan, don't forget your prescription." The woman Kaleene had spoken to earlier came bustling out of the drugstore, waving a small white sack in the air.

He glanced her way, then closed the passenger door firmly. With long strides he met the smiling woman on the edge of the sidewalk. He paused long enough to exchange quick hugs with her before retrieving the sack and returning to the truck. The old engine started without a fuss and Logan carefully backed the Model-T into the quiet street.

Logan. Kaleene ran the name around in her mind, getting the feel of it, trying it out silently on her tongue. It felt deliciously strange.

"I really meant it when I said I was grateful for the ride." Kaleene glanced briefly at his masculine profile.

"Glad to do it."

His short answers were beginning to unnerve her, but the fine sheen of perspiration on her brow was quickly cooling in the gentle breeze blowing through the open windows of the cab. Kaleene forced herself to relax against the back of the seat and turn her attention to their surroundings.

The few short blocks of the business district were behind them now, and they were entering a shady residential section of the small town. Old elm trees, their arching branches stretching high over the brick streets, created a roof of leaves along the way. Clapboard houses, some in comfortable disrepair, others immaculate in appearance, passed sedately by her view as Kaleene gazed fixedly out the open window. The summer air filled with the sweet scent of peaches as they passed a yard bordered in trees heavy with ripening fruit.

Closing her eyes, Kaleene inhaled deeply. "Heavenly."

"What?"

She snapped her eyes open and tried to hide the embarrassed flush of her cheeks as she glanced his way. Logan held the steering wheel with one powerful hand while he kept the other propped on the open window frame. The broad brim of his hat tilted back from his face now, the top barely clearing the rounded roof of the cab.

"This is an interesting truck," she said, trying to appear as calm as he.

A proud smile spread across his handsome face. Tiny creases appeared around his breathtakingly deep blue eyes. "It belonged to my great-granddad."

"You've kept it in remarkable shape." Kaleene found herself mirroring his broad smile. "I suppose you use a different truck for your work?"

"What makes you say that?"

"There's no horseshoeing equipment in the back," she said, looking through the small rear window.

A full-hearted laugh rolled up from his chest and drew her eyes back to him. His blue eyes had taken on a twinkle that she found captivating.

"I only take this truck out on rare occasions."

His eyes lighted on her face, sending a slight shiver up her back. As his eyes drifted back to the street, she felt their absence keenly.

The plaid shirt he wore looked soft, yet durable, she noted. It was the no-nonsense sort of shirt that would belong to a man who worked long, hard hours. The pearl-covered snaps gleamed in their orderly row down his well-defined chest. Logan's jeans looked faded, comfortable.

She stopped studying his clothing and looked up to meet his eyes again. Guiltily she tore her gaze from him and turned to the open window.

"You're quite a detective, miss." He shook his head. "I'm afraid I don't know your name."

"Oh, how silly of me," she exclaimed. "Kaleene." Turning to him, she extended her right hand. "Kaleene LeGare."

Logan switched his grip on the steering wheel and reached across to clasp her slender fingers in his wide palm. So shockingly male, his touch sent her pulse racing.

The world outside faded away in the bright noon sun, like an old photograph, as Kaleene stared at the spot where his flesh pressed its indelible imprint into her tender skin.

"Pleased to meet you"—he paused a moment in his greeting, never releasing his seemingly casual caress of her fingers—"Kaleene." Her name slid from his mouth like silken honey. The slight Texas drawl stretched out the end, somehow making the sound seem so . . . exotic.

A hoarse whisper escaped her lips as she tried to form a response. "I . . . yes." Kaleene pulled her hand away from his scorching touch. "You too," she finally managed.

"We're here." Logan deftly steered the truck to a gentle stop in front of a graceful Victorian two-story home. Tall willows trailed their long branches over a well-manicured lawn that surrounded the inviting wooden structure.

The house seemed to glow with its warm white paint.

when I insisted he get them back in working order instead of plastering over the holes.''

Fannie joined Kaleene on the soft window seat for a good laugh. The older woman's lighthearted nature was infectious.

''This is what I needed.'' Kaleene wiped tears of laughter from her eyes. ''I've missed talking to another woman since . . .''

She couldn't bring herself to say her mother's name. Her death had been so sudden and unexpected. It happened during Kaleene's third year at Purdue's veterinary school. The terrible loss was still too much for her to think about.

Drawing a deep, cleansing breath, Kaleene rose and paced across to the rolltop desk. She ran her fingers lovingly across its polished surface. ''This whole room is just right for me. I've never had a place so lovely. It's almost as if you had me in mind when you decorated it.''

''Well, I've always hoped for a special boarder to come along and fill this room. I've never let it out to our one-nighters, just a few folks who I thought would appreciate its special feel. George has always thought I'm a bit daffy about it.''

Kaleene peered back at Fannie.

''When Doc told me about you, I had a feeling this room would be perfect.''

''Oh, it is! It's marvelous. It's been a long time since I've had a room all to myself,'' she added as she crossed the room and joined Fannie on the window seat again.

''Oh?'' Fannie's eyebrows rose inquisitively.

''Yes,'' Kaleene felt herself opening up. Fannie seemed

to have an ability to make people instantly comfortable with her.

"I shared a dorm room at college for the first two years. Then Mother and I lived in a one-room apartment near campus until—" she shifted her gaze to the ceiling, "until she died. Then I stayed with friends in Fayetteville and Austin until I passed the Texas state board exam and came to work with Dr. Corbin."

"And now you're here with us," Fannie said as she patted Kaleene protectively. "Well, I'd best let you get yourself settled in. I figure you'd want to take a short rest before suppertime. We eat at seven." She rose and crossed to the door. "Doc did tell you that breakfast is served for all the guests, but the full-timers like yourself also eat supper with me and George?"

"Yes. He mentioned that in one of his letters."

"Good. We'll see you and our other full-timer, Miss Hattie, in the kitchen then. Have a good rest." She smiled as she closed the solid door.

Rest! The idea seemed impossible. Excitement sent sparkles of energy up and down her spine. She peered out the window. Much of the small town was visible from her vantage point. A few blocks away the center of town sat amid tree-shrouded neighborhoods. Rising above the other buildings was a square brick building. That must be the courthouse, with its flags visible through the trees.

"That's where I'll start my search," she declared. "As soon as I unpack a few things and change out of these miserably wrinkled clothes."

It seemed a shame to put on her clean clothes without a bath first, and by the time that was done, she felt a few minutes' rest might be a good idea after all. Her visit to the courthouse could wait a little longer, she mused as she lay down. She slept soundly until Fannie woke her at dusk for supper.

The next morning the bright yellow sunlight came streaming in through the windows, creating golden patterns across the white chenille bedspread. Kaleene sat up and pushed her long, honey curls back and eyed her reflection in the round mirror of the antique, drop-center vanity.

"Kaleene, breakfast!" Fannie called as she rapped on the door. Her footsteps faded rapidly away.

This was getting to be a habit, sleeping until Fannie woke her for a meal.

Minutes later she clipped her hair back in a wide, silver butterfly clasp, folding the ends of the intricate hinged combs upward. It was one of the few possessions she had of her mother's. She patted it thoughtfully as a comforted smile lifted her pert features. With a final tug at the waist of her sundress, she went downstairs for breakfast.

"Right there near the end, dear," Fannie said, indicating an empty chair near George.

Eyeing the mounds of steaming waffles, Kaleene slid eagerly into the chair. Conversation was in full swing around the large oak table. There were three new faces this morning.

Last night at the cozy kitchen table, she had met George Smith and Miss Hattie. Kaleene scanned down the table and spotted the quiet form of the frail woman. She sat by Fannie, who chose that moment to dart into the kitchen for some forgotten item.

George poured a tall glass of orange juice and set it in

front of Kaleene. She smiled appreciatively at him and took a sip of the ice-cold juice. It was marvelous, absolutely the best she had tasted, and she wasted no time in telling him so.

He beamed with pride. "Right nice of you to say so. My sweetie pie is tops in the kitchen around these parts. Least, as far as I'm concerned."

"As far as I'm concerned too," Kaleene declared as she nodded her head vigorously. She speared a large waffle from the big platter and began to spread a thick slab of melting butter on it. If the meals continued on this scale she would have to take up some kind of exercise routine.

After such a big meal, she could do nothing but crawl right back into bed. And she dreamed—dreamed of a man in a black cowboy hat. His piercing blue eyes sent her blood singing through her veins. His midnight dark hair had been wild, untamable, whisping from under his hat in all directions. She saw herself reaching up to pull the hat off . . . That was all she remembered.

"Kaleene."

Startled out of her private thoughts, Kaleene glanced around the table.

"You going to Doc's place this morning?" Fannie asked.

"I'm not expected to report to work for another week, but I thought I might go by and say hello later. After breakfast, I plan to take a walk downtown."

"Well, you need to find any place in particular, you just ask my George. He can give right good directions."

Kaleene smiled at the woman's kindness. Having these good people to rely on would make her life in Tumbleweed much easier. With the hard task she faced, Kaleene feared that she would need their support very much. The first step to completing that task lay at the courthouse, and she suddenly felt eager to get started.

"You be sure to get your walking done before the mercury climbs too high," George advised her. "Best you leave going to Doc's till late afternoon sometime. He'll be there—always is," he announced cheerfully.

Kaleene took his advice to heart and set out in the direction of the cluster of businesses shortly after breakfast. She knew now that the courthouse was only a block away from the drugstore where she had arrived yesterday. Glimpses of the imposing gray structure came through the trees as she drew near the building.

Outside on the lawn, she paused. Finally she was in reach of a place where she could get some answers. After all these years she would be able to add to the little scraps of knowledge she held so dear.

Chapter Two

Kaleene felt exhausted. A fine film of gray dust covered her from head to toe. It streaked her tired arms and clung to her limp hair.

In the tiled washroom of the courthouse she scrubbed her grimy hands. The refreshing, cool water ran down her arms as she attempted to clean the worst of the dust from her exposed skin.

There had been boxes and boxes of old files to go through. The records, meticulously labeled, had been stored with care in a small room of the dusty basement. She had spent hours poring through each one, learning a great deal about the founding of Tumbleweed and Drover County along the way. Names, dates, it was more than she needed, more than she wanted to know about her new home.

But, she smiled at herself in the tiny mirror over the pedestal sink, she had found something. It was just a small

19

scrap of information, but it might lead to more clues. She glanced over to the counter where her straw purse and small notebook sat.

Confidently Kaleene dried her hands and face and smoothed her rumpled hair back. After a quick combing she bound the now organized honey-colored mass at the nape of her neck. The drier air of Texas had done wonders for the managability of her much-disdained natural curl.

The smudges on her dress wouldn't disappear completely, despite her vigorous efforts with a damp paper towel. At least she no longer looked like such a mess.

She gathered her things and quickly made her way into the bright noon sun. A steady breeze cooled her bare arms and dried the dampened spots of her dress.

It would be only a short walk to the sandwich shop across from the drugstore. Kaleene decided to have a sand wich while she thought about her newfound information.

A few customers occupied the cane-backed stools at the counter that ran the length of the shop. Some of them gave her a casual glance when she entered. Kaleene seated herself at one of the round tables of the quaint sandwich shop. Her waitress was a very young, blond girl, probably the daughter of the trim brunet who busily prepared platters of food in the small, open kitchen.

"What would you recommend?" Kaleene asked the eager young girl as she took the hand-lettered menu. The stiff linen paper was a light coral color, with roses sketched in blue ink across the top.

"Mom's crab salad is terrific. Or you might try the club sandwich. I like that, followed by a big piece of apple pie."

Kaleene smiled appreciatively at the girl who emphasized the word *big* with a widening of her eyes as she held her hands out in the air about a foot apart.

"My!" Kaleene marveled. "That does sound tempting. A club sandwich and apple pie it is!"

The girl grinned in approval. "How about a glass of iced tea to go with it?"

"That would be perfect."

As she waited for her order she pulled the notebook from her purse. The textured, dark brown leather cover felt warm and reassuring under her fingers. Written inside were the coordinates of a piece of land. Now the next step was to locate that land. It should be easy enough to do.

What she needed now was a map. Should her next stop be a gas station, or a bookstore? She had no idea where to find either place.

The young waitress came to the table, carrying her order, and Kaleene quickly slipped the notebook back in her purse. "Thank you." She flashed the waitress a genuine smile.

"You're welcome." The young girl smiled back, her dimpled cheeks flushed. "My name's Mary. If there's anything else you need, just call me." She swiftly returned to her mother's side.

As Kaleene watched her walking away she caught the twinkling eye of Mary's mother. The two women exchanged broad smiles, Mary's mother's full of pride, Kaleene's full of the loving memories she had of her own mother.

A tiny, two-room apartment on the second floor of a rundown apartment building in a poorer part of Chicago had been her home for all of her childhood. Her mother worked hard to pay for food and rent. But that wasn't where the family had lived when Kaleene was born.

Then, home was a charming little house in a quiet suburb of Chicago. Shortly after Kaleene's birth, her father lost his job. The pressure of supporting his wife and child with what little income he could make on the occasional odd job eventually proved too much for him. One day he simply didn't come home.

At first, her mother feared he'd been injured in an accident. She scoured the hospitals in the area with no luck. Then, she reluctantly filed a missing person report at the local police station. After several weeks, the police had turned up no trace of him. Soon, growing tired of taking her many calls, a detective callously told her he probably got fed up with having the burden of a family and simply ran off. Many husbands did that, he said. She should get on with her life and forget the man.

But she couldn't. They had a home, a loving marriage, and a beautiful child. He would come back, she convinced herself. So she hung on to her hope, day by day, waiting for a man who would never return.

Eventually the house was repossessed for the unpaid mortgage. She had no family to turn to. With the help of volunteers from the Salvation Army, she moved with her six-month-old daughter into the tiny apartment in Chicago. Her mother finally realized the truth. Her husband would never return. They were alone.

With no education, piecework at a nearby clothing manufacturer was the best job she could find. One important adjustment she made to bolster her self-confidence was to take back her maiden name, and she had Kaleene's changed as well.

In her early years, Kaleene stayed with a variety of neighbors and sitters. But the evenings were what she remembered most about those hard times. Her mother always had a happy expression when she retrieved Kaleene at the end of the workday.

Their shabby place would take on a marvelous quality as soon as Kaleene's mother shut the front door. The cold, hard floor had been covered with colorful scraps of carpet from a local thrift shop. Bright curtains made of fabric remnants covered the windows. Kaleene had several rag dolls made from strange and exotic print scraps her mother brought home from work.

Somehow, the most tedious of chores got turned into a wonderful adventure. Their plain food always assumed the most outlandish names. Laundry chores were always accompanied by fun songs and counting games.

As Kaleene grew older, she began to ask questions, questions about her father. At first they were simple, easy questions. But as she began to get less satisfied with the short answers she received, her questions grew more probing.

The story of his leaving came out bit by bit, but her mother was never able to explain why he left, not in a way that a teenage girl could understand. But her mother always ended their talks with a promise, that Kaleene would have a good education. That was her way of guaranteeing that her daughter would never go through this with her own child.

A college education meant scrimping and saving for the next several years, scholarships to apply for when the time came, and the one thing that turned out to be easy, high grades for Kaleene.

During her high-school years, Kaleene worked hard and graduated valedictorian. Her mother sat in the large auditorium, her eyes shining with pride and watched what some of her coworkers said was a miracle. But she knew Kaleene's success was the product of love and hard work.

The following month, they moved for the second time in their lives. Saying good-bye to the close friends they made in the poor neighborhood had been hard. There were people whom they had relied on through difficult times, and people who had relied on them. There were many tears shed the bright, summer day she and her mother left on their exciting bus ride to Lafayette, Indiana.

George was right about walking in the midday heat. with directions to the bookstore from Mary's mother, Kaleene stepped out of the sandwich shop and instantly decided the hunt for a map could wait. She turned in the direction of the Smiths' inn.

The shaded streets were wonderfully peaceful as Kaleene walked leisurely back home. That was probably why she felt so startled when a shiny, metallic blue pickup pulled up to the corner she was approaching and the driver tapped its horn. Logan's strikingly handsome face appeared as he rolled down the window.

"Hey, how about a lift?" he called.

She almost laughed. There was only one short block between her and home. The deep green of the inn's willows was already visible.

"It's a lot cooler in here," he said bribing her with a dimpled grin.

With what she hoped looked like a casual shrug of her shoulder, she crossed the quiet street and met him as he quickly scrambled out. Gallantly he ushered her around to the passenger door and held it wide as she climbed inside. With a few tugs at the full skirt of her cotton sundress, Kaleene was settled almost primly before Logan slid his lanky frame back behind the wheel of the shiny truck.

"This can't be a truck anybody uses for farrier work," she declared. Her eyes shone a challenge at the well-built man seated beside her.

"All right," he said, sighing in exasperation. "How'd you guess?"

"It's too clean."

Logan gaped at her for a moment, almost as if he were unsure if he should take her words as a compliment or a further challenge. Finally a twinkle of amusement shone through the midnight blue of his intense gaze.

"Well, it could be that I'm just extremely neat."

Kaleene clamped a hand hastily over her parted lips to contain the laughter that she felt building inside.

A mock look of dismay spread from Logan's eyebrows downward to cover his well-defined features.

Kaleene shook her head. She had seen too many farriers at work to believe this was a truck used to haul around their various tools of the trade.

"All right," he finally acquiesced. "I do see your point. I don't think any farrier could keep his working truck in this kind of shape."

"Thank you." Kaleene accepted his admission of defeat as graciously as he tendered it.

"Now, perhaps we can get going?" Logan waved his sun-tanned hand in the direction of the street. "But not before I ask you if home is really where you were going."

"Well, I was going back to wait out the heat of the day before walking over to Dr. Corbin's office."

Logan flashed her a wide grin. "How about a short ride first? A little sightseeing to let you get a feel for your new home?"

Kaleene contemplated the short cushioned bench seat, the cool air-conditioning blowing strongly from the small vents along the padded dash, and finally, the man waiting confidently beside her.

"All right," she exclaimed quickly before any second thoughts could form.

In just a few short blocks they were out of the little community and speeding down narrow farming roads. The line of asphalt stretched on for endless miles, never curving, only dipping and rising occasionally. Logan changed their direction sporadically when they intersected another road that, to Kaleene, looked exactly like the one they just left.

"Isn't the legal speed limit still fifty-five miles an hour in Texas?" Kaleene asked, her voice echoing with the concern she felt as she saw the speed with which the scenery rushed by.

"Speed limit? I don't think we have such a thing around these parts as a speed limit." Logan shook his head in dismay at the very idea of such a thing.

"Well, maybe you should slow down a bit anyway,"

Kaleene stated flatly. "I seem to be missing all the good scenery. Seeing the sights is why you brought me out here, isn't it?"

"Oh, yes," Logan declared, straight-faced. "All the grand forests, rivers, and lakes," he added, sweeping his arm across the empty, flat horizon.

But he did slow down, she noted as she followed his grand gesture with her eyes. Gently rolling plains covered with green fields of ripening wheat stretched ahead on both sides of the straight road.

"I never realized land could go on for so long."

Logan regarded her thoughtfully for a moment.

"I mean, it's almost too vast to comprehend. Don't you think so?" she asked, turning to him for confirmation.

His lips—she couldn't keep her eyes from drifting down to them—were curled slightly up at the very corners. A hint of his dimples showed.

"Yes. I know what you're talking about. It was the first thing I noticed when I came back home from college."

"You went to college?" To Kaleene's utter mortification she recognized a note of surprise in her voice. A loud note. "I meant—" She thought furiously for a second. "I meant to ask what college you went to."

"Texas A & M," he supplied. The slight smile broadened as he drilled her with his blue gaze.

"Oh, how nice. Is it here in Texas?"

"Yes," he replied levelly. "Texas A & M is here in Texas."

Now she felt like a complete idiot. He must think her an absolute dolt. But it wasn't her fault. He had her so flustered. Kaleene fixed her gaze out the front window as her restless hands knotted together in her lap.

"What are those long pipes on wheels sitting out in the field?" she asked, desperate to fill the silence.

"That's a drop-line irrigation system. But you don't really want to talk about that, do you?"

Oh, yes. She was ready to discuss anything if it helped cover her nervousness.

"I was wondering if you'd tell me more about yourself," Logan said as he shifted around toward her and laid his right arm along the back of the bench seat.

"Now, that's really a subject that's boring," she declared.

"I see. So are you leaving it up to me to decide on what we talk about?" His tone was amused, and somehow challenging at the same time.

"I suppose." She seemed to surrender. "But could I make a small suggestion?"

"Sure." He waved his hand magnanimously, inches from her long curls.

"You might tell me a bit about where we're going." She arched her brows, returning his challenge.

Logan rocked his head back with delighted laughter. His wide-brimmed Stetson hat tipped against the rear window. His eyes sparkled as he said, "I'm saving that as a surprise. But I will fill you in a bit on your new home."

Kaleene watched him in concealed amazement as he spun what surely must be invented yarns about his friends and neighbors who inhabited the plains around the quiet, close-knit community of Tumbleweed.

He was in the middle of a ludicrous tale of a neighbor's

wandering heifer when the truck topped a rise. Kaleene caught sight of a lone, two-story farmhouse about a mile west of the road they traveled down. She stared intently at the structure as they drew closer to it.

The place appeared deserted. She could see tumbleweeds almost choking the long, winding sandy drive that had become deeply rutted by the torrential rains that whipped across the area each spring. The house, with its white, wooden siding showing signs of chipping and peeling paint, looked lonely. Sun-bleached curtains covered the upstairs windows, and of the downstairs windows Kaleene could see only the dreary, green shutters.

A small barn, slightly sagging, stood several yards behind the house. Green paint barely showed on its trim. Near the screened side porch, a windmill, its metal blades dull and still, stood like a silent sentinel.

The place looked so familiar . . . could she have seen it before? No. That was ridiculous. She'd never been here before in her life. Kaleene twisted around and stared thoughtfully out the back window at the forlorn house as it retreated in the distance. As the truck crested another rise and sank down the other side she lost sight of the hauntingly familiar place.

Countless turns later Logan pulled through a gate that proclaimed the land they entered to be a wildlife preserve.

"Not just any preserve," he pointed out to her. "The Muleshoe National Wildlife Preserve." He leaned around the steering wheel and reached a well-muscled arm under the truck's seat.

Green binoculars, almost as long as her forearm, were

what he pulled out. He uncapped the lenses and handed them to her.

As he pulled the pickup to the edge of a shallow, wet area, she squinted through the lenses. Lush, green grasses bordered the water. Clumps of reeds dotted the shoreline. There was so much to look at, she tried taking the sights in all at once, but found her mind overloaded with it all.

Her thoughts, freed momentarily by her inability to concentrate, drifted back to the house they had passed. There were many other houses very similar they had passed that day. Most were located near windmills. But something had struck a chord in her. . . .

"—sandhill cranes."

Logan's last words penetrated Kaleene's distracted mind. "Sandhill cranes?" she asked.

"Earlier in the year, of course," he continued, unaware of her confusion.

"What is?"

"Their mating season," he replied, now aware that somewhere in his explanation of what he'd brought her here to see her attention had wandered. "For a vet, you're not much into wildlife, are you?"

The accusing words stung her. Unable to form a coherent response amid the sudden irritation, Kaleene swung the heavy binoculars away from her eyes and fixed a glare on her face. But Logan was smiling at her.

It was another of those dazzling, toothy grins that he was so good at. It seemed to draw her forward into the golden aura that Logan emanated around himself.

"Let's take a short hike along that trail," he said, pointing to a smooth path near the edge of the clearing they parked in.

Kaleene eagerly followed him through the tall grasses as he pointed out birds that were feeding around them. He showed her blooms of wildflowers, swaying cattails, and a lone cotton plant that must have resulted from a seed blown here from a farmer's field.

They stopped, sheltering in the shade of a short mesquite tree, while Logan described trips he had taken here as a boy. Kaleene envied him. This was such a wonderful place to grow up in. So much for a child to do, so many places to go. She thought back to her childhood. How much happier she and her mother would have been, living here.

A cool breeze ruffled loose tendrils of her hair across her face, and Kaleene turned to face the western sky. Thin lines of clouds were gradually appearing, stretching across the western horizon. The tip on one white band crept up until it barely touched the edge of the sun. Its whiteness turned a deep, golden red.

"It's getting late," she said reluctantly. Definitely too late for that visit she had planned to make to the clinic. She'd save that for tomorrow. But it was time to return to the bed-and-breakfast, she unwillingly admitted to herself. "I should be getting back."

He hesitated for a moment, then gently took her hand and led her back to the pickup.

"He invited me to a barn dance this Friday at the Lawford ranch." Kaleene shook her head in dismay as she complained to Fannie that evening in the kitchen. A smooth layer of cookie dough sat on the cutting board in front of her. Kaleene began pressing a mason jar lid into the raw mixture of pecan sandies.

Fannie pulled a hot cookie sheet from the oven. "And what's so terrible about that? Logan's a fine man, and it's always a fun evening when the Lawfords have their annual barn dance." She smiled and winked at Kaleene as she dusted her hands on a gingham apron.

"I have absolutely no idea what to wear!" Kaleene furiously ground the lid into the dough, giving it an extra twisting motion for good measure.

"Let me see." Fannie picked up a spatula and began transferring the cooling cookies to an already heaping plate. "Last summer I recall seeing a lot of folks in jeans and boots at the Lawfords' dance. And quite a few in skirts. I reckon whatever you choose'll be just right."

"Well, I do have a really full denim skirt. . . ."

"That sounds perfect!" Fannie beamed as she began loading Kaleene's round shapes onto the cookie sheet.

"I could wear it with a white blouse, and maybe tie my hair back with a blue bandanna." She tapped her fingers thoughtfully against the counter.

"You'll be pretty as a picture," Fannie declared.

Kaleene's eyes shone as she smiled at her new friend and confidante. "You and George will be there?" she asked hopefully.

"Sure enough. But Logan'll keep you too busy to visit with old folks like us."

"Fannie!" Kaleene scolded the laughing woman, then gave her a hug, leaving floury handprints on her shoulders.

The sky had a crystalline turquoise quality the next morning when Kaleene set out for Dr. Corbin's office.

From there, she planned to take a short stroll to the town center to pick up a map at the bookstore.

She'd dressed in a light cotton blouse and shorts. Not the most professional image for meeting the doctor, she mused, but this was only to be a short visit. This would be the first time she would be speaking to him face-to-face, but she felt she knew what to expect of him. They had exchanged many letters and several phone calls while finalizing their agreement.

She remembered the trepidation she'd felt answering the ad for a veterinarian that she'd seen on the college bulletin board. Many graduating students got their jobs through these ads placed by potential employers. Kaleene remembered scanning down the list many times. Then one day her eye caught on the name of the town, Tumbleweed, Texas, the same as the postmark on the letter from her father.

It took almost a week for her to work up the courage to answer the ad. She promptly received a reply from Dr. Corbin stating that he liked her qualification and was eager to hear if she was agreeable to the terms of a partnership he outlined in the letter. He hoped that she would eventually take over the business when he retired; the terms had been more than generous, requiring no money from her, just work.

Kaleene reached the end of the block and caught sight of the highway that ran along the northern border of the community of Tumbleweed. Dr. Corbin's animal clinic was just across from her.

As she drew near, she studied the wide, squat building. The clean, white cinder-block structure, with narrow windows across the front, stood alone in a large parking lot. The lot seemed absurdly large, until Kaleene realized it needed to accommodate trucks pulling livestock trailers. Much of Dr. Corbin's practice was in large animals. That made perfect sense in this region.

In the rear, a fence extended from both sides of the building to enclose two metal sheds and a tidy kennel. A few trees bordered the west side, providing shade for all of the fenced area.

A tiny, silver bell above the front door rang merrily as she entered. A tall brunet, not much older than Kaleene, perched on a stool behind the counter, busily filing her candy-apple red nails. Her hair was teased and sprayed into one of the tallest creations Kaleene had ever seen.

"Hey y'all."

Oh, that distinctly southern greeting. Kaleene smiled at the young woman. "Hi. I'm looking for Dr. Corbin. Would he be in?"

"Oh, sure, hon. The doc's in, but he's a mite busy at the moment. Got a touchy young bullock out back."

Kaleene drew nearer the counter and leaned on it for support. "I'm Kaleene LeGare—"

"You are?" she almost shouted in her excitement. "Doc's been waiting for you!"

Kaleene plugged a finger in her offended eardrum. The receptionist, oblivious to what her loud tone had done, continued on with her tirade as she jumped off her stool and swooped around the counter. She grabbed Kaleene by the arm and pulled her through the back of the building.

"He told me all about you. Said you were getting in

sometime next week. But it's great you're here early cause I'm the only one helping him now that summer's here. You're pretty young to be a vet and all. Right about my age, aren't you?''

"I'm twenty-five. I suppose . . ." Kaleene's reply was drowned out as they passed through a room of cages. Two large dogs, a collie and a German shepherd, set up a cacophony of barking.

The receptionist banged open the rear door and pulled Kaleene outside. "Now we just might need to be a little quiet, you know? The doc treating that bullock and all. He probably wouldn't take kindly to the creature being riled up or nothing."

Tucked in a corner of the tidy, fenced area was a small paddock fenced in sturdy pipe. Inside it, Kaleene caught sight of a small, grizzled man in a beat-up straw hat, hunched down next to a young bull. The animal stood tied to a rail, foraging in a bucket resting on the ground.

She tried to study the man, but her eyes were drawn instinctively to the injured animal. A shallow cut showed on his right foreleg, about six inches long, running at a slight angle. Dr. Corbin had finished cleaning the wound and was now preparing to bandage it.

"Do-oc, Do-oc," the receptionist softly called, her voice barely above a whisper.

As the man turned his tanned, wrinkled face to peer over his shoulder at her, she exclaimed, "She's here!" in as loud a voice as she had used inside.

The bullock, as startled as Kaleene was by the woman's screeching voice, jerked his head up suddenly, upsetting the pail and spilling its contents all around his feet. Dr. Corbin, cursing loudly, scrambled about trying to rescue his supplies as the young bull danced to and fro at the end of its tether.

Chapter Three

"I wasn't expecting you until next week, but I certainly won't complain about the help." Doc, as he insisted she call him, showed Kaleene around the animal clinic. He had donned a blue lab coat when they finished bandaging the bullock's leg and reentered the building.

"I was glad to help." Kaleene followed him from his cluttered office down the short hall into a small room.

"This'll be yours. Sam rounded up the desk for me," he said, indicating a well-worn oak desk. It sat against the large window that faced the parking lot, its drawers against the glass. " 'Course, you might want to rearrange things a bit."

Kaleene turned back to the door as his voice faded away. She scrambled into the hall and caught sight of his coattail vanishing through another doorway. Quickly she jogged down the hall and skidded to an abrupt halt as he stuck his gray head back out.

"That's where you got to! Try not to get lost from now on."

Startled by his gruff manner, she followed closely on his heels for the rest of the tour. They took a quick inventory of supplies, checked the condition of several pieces of equipment, and finished the tour by checking the health of a mother dog and her litter of new pups brought in by an anxious red-haired boy and his dad. The puppies and mother were sent home with a clean bill of health.

"Lunch!" screeched the receptionist, whose name Kaleene finally learned was Velma. "Doc, you going out, or you want me to bring you something? I'll bring you something too, Doc LeGare!"

Doc LeGare. Kaleene felt the horrible sound of that echo around in her head. The way Velma drew out her last name was atrocious. It came out sounding more like two separate words. Lee Gair. Ugh.

When Logan said her name with his soft, southern drawl, the sound had done wonderful things to her ears. The sensual way his mouth formed around the sounds, and the sweet way the tones rolled from his lips . . . It sent a shiver up her spine simply to think about it.

"Bring me back my usual," Doc said, scowling at Velma as she stuck her head in his office door. He sat at his desk behind several piles of forms and folders, discussing ordering procedures for drugs and supplies.

"And you?"

"Oh, thanks, Velma, but I'll get something when Doc and I finish here."

"You'll do no such thing," he said, fuming. "Won't have you keeling over from malnourishment before you've even started working." Waving down her protest, Dr. Corbin commanded Velma to bring Kaleene something good and nourishing. "She needs more meat on those bones!"

Kaleene eyed the strong-willed man for a moment. Had she made a mistake coming here to a new work environment, hundreds of miles from all her friends, and not knowing a single soul?

Doc glowered back at her, daring her to defy his edict. His letters had only let her know so much about the man. But she had expected him to be a caring individual who valued other people's feelings. He'd seemed kind and considerate on the phone, like he'd been with the boy and his new puppies, Kaleene reflected.

The child was worried. It was his dog's first litter and to him, the new puppies looked impossibly small and helpless. Their pink noses seemed so vulnerable, and their heads so wobbly. He feared they wouldn't be able to eat, to grow big and healthy like their mother. But Doc checked each pup carefully, taking extra time to answer every question the young boy asked.

Then the elderly vet had Velma bring a book from his office. It was full of pictures of newborn puppies. The boy and Doc sat on the floor by the box of puppies, poring over the pictures, page after page, until the young master felt satisfied. Doc helped carry the box back to the family station wagon and saw them all settled safely in the back with the mother dog.

This gruff old man, wizened and wrinkled, was all porcupine on the outside, but Kaleene had seen through that image he projected. She had made a good choice to come here. This was where her search led her, and more than that, she was beginning to realize this was a place she could belong.

Kaleene returned his stern glare, her posture now just as stiff as his.

"That is," he paused to clear his throat, "if you don't mind eating with a tough old bird like me?"

She held her lips in their grim line until his look softened. "I'd love to have lunch with you, Doc. Thanks for the invitation."

He cleared his throat again, muffling the soft tittering noise Velma made as she vanished from the doorway.

Friday morning the sun seemed to rise earlier than usual. Kaleene rolled over and sank farther into the feather mattress. Outside her window a warbling mockingbird flitted around in the trailing branches of the lush, green willow trees. This would be her fifth day in Tumbleweed, and she still hadn't made it to the bookstore for that map. Today would definitely be the day, she swore to herself.

She sat up and looked at the faded wedding picture in its silver frame and the stack of papers on the little marbletop table by the bed. Last night she had stayed up late mulling over the few bits of information she had—clues really, clues about her father.

Kaleene lifted the crinkled paper from the top of the too-short pile. After seventeen years he had finally written his family a letter. It arrived shortly after her seventeenth birthday.

The stunned look on her mother's face was still vivid in

her mind. After all those years, to finally hear from him ... It had taken her mother days to get over the shock of receiving the letter.

"Kaleene," Fannie called cheerfully as she tapped on the bedroom door.

A powder blue satin robe lay draped across the foot of her bed. Kaleene pulled it on as she padded barefoot to the door.

"Didn't wake you, did I, hon?" Fannie asked as Kaleene welcomed her into the sunny room.

"Oh, no. I've been lying awake in bed for quite some time. It's so lovely in here in the morning light." Kaleene stretched her supple frame as she strolled over to the four-poster bed and smoothed the covers in place. She took extra care in straightening the soft, chenille spread.

"Yes. It's a glorious morning," Fannie said, sighing contentedly as she gazed out the wide windows.

Kaleene sat before the vanity and busied herself with brushing her hair back into its usual lustrous curls.

"I've been planning on going out to my cousin's place after breakfast," Fannie said as she sat by the bright view. "She's got some blueberries ripening. Thought you might like to come along."

"How very thoughtful of you to invite me. I would love to." Kaleene smiled at her in the mirror.

"Fine then. We'll get going as soon as I get the kitchen squared away. Be sure you bring a hat."

"I will," Kaleene promised as she tied her curling hair back with a bright pink ribbon.

"That your folks?"

Kaleene glanced sharply at Fannie's reflection once

more. She had moved over to the marble table and was studying the photograph.

"Yes," she answered reluctantly, then continued more easily, "my mom and dad on their wedding day. She was so happy then. She looks so carefree there." Kaleene crossed the room and picked up the framed picture.

"You take after your mother quite a bit."

Kaleene smiled in gratitude. "That's lovely of you to say. We were very close. More like pals, I suppose."

"Is that right? And your pop?" Fannie asked.

A troubled look clouded Kaleene's face as she stared down at the photo cradled in her hands. "He left my mom soon after I was born." She worked to swallow the lump that rose in her throat. "We heard that he died a year after I entered college. A notice from the I.R.S.; Mom was due some money. It was a difficult way to hear the news."

"They made a right handsome couple. It's a shame you never got to be with him." Fannie patted her shoulder comfortingly.

"We did receive a message from him once."

Fannie's supportive smile encouraged Kaleene to continue. "He wrote us a letter, apologizing for leaving us. He said he knew we would never be able to understand why he had done it, but he needed to know that we could forgive him."

"That's all the contact you had with him?"

"Yes. That letter was all. He told us a little about his life, about the house he lived in."

She returned to the bench in front of the vanity. There was an image in her mind, one she'd carried for the last few years. Her father's house. It closely resembled the house she'd seen during that ride with Logan. She had been shocked last night when she reread the letter and realized the similarities. But she had seen many other houses that day that might have fit the same general description.

"It took Mom a long time to come to terms with his resurfacing in her life. We never discussed him much after that. Eventually she gave me this photograph." She returned to the table and set the picture down and picked up the letter. "I've treasured the picture and this letter ever since her death."

And now her search for more knowledge of him had led her here to Tumbleweed, Texas. That was something she would tell no one. Not even Fannie.

"Your mother must have loved him deeply to have kept the picture all those years."

"Yes, I believe she did." Squaring her shoulders and clearing her mind of all those bittersweet memories, Kaleene addressed Fannie, "Now, about those blueberries . . ."

Discreetly she tucked the letter under the pile of papers on the table, hiding the postmark that read Tumbleweed, Texas.

Kaleene felt exhausted and happy by the time she and Fannie returned late that afternoon. They had picked berries—and eaten too many, until their arms ached and their stomachs threatened rebellion. Fannie's sister insisted they eat lunch with her and her three grandkids. The kitchen had been full of chatter and good food, but Kaleene was glad to be back home.

Home. The inn really was becoming home, the first place

she had felt that way about since that tiny little apartment in Lafayette, Indiana, she shared with her mother.

The water gurgled in the clawfoot bathtub as Kaleene undressed. What she needed was a good, relaxing soak before getting ready for the dance tonight with Logan. She added a lavender-scented bath foam to the running water and swirled it around in lazy circles before sinking chin-deep into the exquisite feel of the warm liquid. The deep, cast-iron tub, with its gently sloping back, gave her wonderful support as the strains of the day seeped from her body. A rolled hand towel served wonderfully as a pillow, and soon her eyes drifted shut.

Tonight she would see Logan again. How incredible it all seemed. She had only met him five days ago, and there hadn't been more than an hour during any of those days when he wasn't in her thoughts. At least, it seemed that way. Even today, when she was picking berries, thoughts of him stole into her mind. Did he like blueberries as much as she did?

Later, when she and Fannie stopped by the bookstore, Kaleene found herself staring down the street toward the drugstore, remembering that first meeting with Logan there. She had almost left without her map!

Tonight would definitely be a special time. Kaleene reluctantly left the tub, but only after the water grew too chilled. She toweled herself dry and unwrapped her still-damp hair. After applying a light mousse she allowed it to air-dry. That always gave her natural curls a nice bounce.

Kaleene descended the stairs in her full denim skirt and simple white blouse. A blue bandanna kept her long hair away from her face, but allowed it to be loose and flowing down her back. She felt like a debutante going to her first ball. The giddy thought brought a smile to her face.

At the bottom of the wide staircase, Fannie and George waited to give their stamp of approval to her. She grinned self-consciously but they smiled back so broadly, she couldn't help laughing. Miss Hattie came through the parlor doors and joined the Smiths.

"Mighty pretty, mighty pretty," George declared to the two women at his side. "She looks just right to me."

"Not quite," Fannie objected, causing her husband to snicker conspiratorially. "There appears to be one thing wrong."

Kaleene stopped on the bottom step, looking down at her clothing, then eyeing the little group suspiciously.

Fannie stepped closer and brought her hands from behind her back. She held a pair of red cowboy boots. They shone like new, yet didn't seem to have the stiffness of unworn boots. There was a slight curl to the toe and a few creases around the ankles that indicated they'd been worn, but lovingly taken care of.

"Go on," Fannie urged as she held them out to Kaleene. "They're a gift. Calfskin Ropers, and I happen to know they're just your size."

"Oh, no. I couldn't. I mean, these are yours, aren't they? I couldn't take them."

" 'Course you can, girl," George reassured her. "They were Fannie's, sure enough. But she's got more pairs than you can shake a stick at. Besides, this'll give her a good excuse to get one more pair. But"—he turned and walked toward the kitchen muttering to himself—"that is one woman who sure don't need an excuse to buy more clothes or shoes. If there ever was a woman who had more stuff in her closet than my Fannie . . .''

''They'll go a whole lot better than those loafers,'' Fannie said, pointing at Kaleene's shoes. Miss Hattie shook her white head vigorously in agreement, dislodging thin wisps of hair from her bun.

Kaleene took the boots and immediately gave Fannie the most heartfelt hug she could. ''Thank you,'' she whispered past the lump in her throat. The gift was a gesture straight from the heart and Kaleene tried to let Fannie know how much it meant to her.

The three women moved to the parlor where Fannie had laid out a pair of socks to go with the boots. Perched on a low stool, Kaleene pulled the boots on. They fit perfectly.

As George returned to the parlor and joined his wife in admiring the boots, a rowdy knock rattled the front door. It was Logan, exactly on time.

Chapter Four

Pickup trucks of all sizes and colors, Suburbans, Broncos, and even a few sedans lined both sides of the long, curving drive of the stately Lawford home. Walking up the unpaved drive, with her arm firmly linked in Logan's, Kaleene was again grateful for the beautiful red boots. They took a little getting used to, she had to admit. With the narrow toe, and tight heel inherent in the design, they would have to be a good fit to be comfortable. But Fannie had been right about the size.

Kaleene found herself glancing down repeatedly at her feet as she and Logan drew nearer the noise and light emanating from the tall, red structure by the split-level ranch house. She was consciously taking longer strides, feeling the way her foot rolled on the rounded back of the heel, then forward on the slightly curved-up toe. The smooth, cool leather of the boot top brushed back and forth against

47

her bare calf with each step. It was almost a sensual caress, further reminding her of the strangeness of wearing cowboy boots. The hem of her denim skirt ended about six inches above the boot tops, revealing just a little of her bare legs. It was a marvelous feeling and she reveled in it.

Logan smiled enticingly at Kaleene. "Great boots."

Her cheeks flushed. "They're a gift from Fannie."

He nodded his head and held her closer as they stepped through a wide circle of hay bales outlining the clearing in front of the barn's open doors. A few of the guests were sitting on the gold bales, chatting. Paper lanterns hung from the tall oak trees, casting yellow glows in the gathering darkness.

Passing through the doorway into the well-lit barn and directly into the press of milling people, Kaleene caught sight of a country-and-western band at the other end of the seemingly vast wooden structure. The musicians were on a raised platform and in full swing. Two fiddlers in matching turquoise shirts stood side by side at the front of the stage, playing fast and furiously. The fringe trim on their shirts danced about with their vigorous movements.

"Is it too loud in here for you?" Logan asked.

"No. I love it." She had to raise her voice a bit to be heard.

Logan smiled and ushered her deeper inside. Several people waved a greeting to Logan or tapped his shoulder as he passed. He led her to a stop at the edge of a hardwood floor occupied by couples. They were stepping and twirling in intricate country-and-western dance steps.

Kaleene froze at Logan's side, her eyes riveted on the dancers. She had no idea how to do that! How could it have never occurred to her before this moment that a barn dance would mean country-and-western dancing? Her hand reflexively convulsed its grip on Logan's arm.

Peripherally she was aware that he had been exchanging greetings with someone to his left. At her involuntary tug on his arm, he immediately turned his captivating blue eyes to her vividly scarlet face.

"Is the crush too much for you?" His mouth brushed against her ear as he tried to make himself understood while trying to keep his words private.

The overwhelming closeness of Logan was too much for her, not the crowd. She pressed her lips in a thin line and regarded him apprehensively. Yes. He was the reason she hadn't thought about what type of dancing there would be here. The only thoughts she'd had were of being with him again. Nothing else had mattered.

He slipped his sinewy arm around her waist, holding her firmly in the protective circle of his embrace. "Let's step outside," he said.

Kaleene parted her lips, intent on denying her unease. "Logan—"

"Logan!" A slim teenage girl with hair as jet dark as his tugged on his shirt. "Logan, I thought you'd never get here. Clay's dad is letting all the kids go up to the house and play pool and stuff in his den. Juanita said I couldn't go till I asked you." She held her hands out in an exasperated gesture.

"How nice to see you using such lovely manners, Sis." His furrowed brow said he was anything but pleased by her behavior.

"Sorry," she muttered, her eyes downcast.

"Kaleene, I'd like to introduce my little sister, Denice—"

"Denny!" The girl stamped her foot as she sternly corrected his version of her name.

"Sorry," he echoed his sister with arched brows. "Denny—" he began, only to be interrupted by her again.

"Nice to meet you." Denny shot her hand out and pumped Kaleene's in greeting as she continued to speak. "Logan, can I go, please? All the other kids are already up at the house. I've got to go right now, or else..." She paused and glanced furtively about at the people crowded nearby. "Well, there won't be anybody left worth talking to."

Overwhelmed by Denny's badgering, Logan sighed and motioned for her to go.

"Oh, thanks, big brother." Denny tiptoed to plant a quick kiss on Logan's cheek, then fled through the crowd.

Logan removed his hat and rifled through his thick black hair, shaking his head at Denny's hasty departure. "I suppose the 'anybody worth talking to' is young Clay. That girl's in for a heartache."

"Is he interested in someone else?" Kaleene glanced from the door that Denny had disappeared through to Logan's troubled eyes.

"Well, I think it's more a case of him not even knowing she's alive. Fifteen-year-old girls are a little beneath his notice. He's a senior this year. If there was some way I could protect her feelings..."

Logan planted his hat firmly on his head again and wrapped his arm back around her waist, his hip brushing against hers. "We were just about to move out of the crowd, weren't we?"

He guided her to the side of the barn near long tables laden with food and drink. Several members of a uniformed catering staff were adding to the trays of lobster and roast beef, or helping guests to the sparkling champagne and red wines. Kaleene could see barbecued chicken and long-necked bottles of beer. There was something here for everyone, no matter what their tastes were.

"How about a little something to eat?" he asked. "We could grab a couple of plates and join the folks on the hay bales outside."

"It all looks delicious," she said, working hard to appear at ease. "But maybe we could sit and talk awhile first."

"Sounds great," he said with a decisive nod.

She matched his stride as they made their way past the food and drink to a row of chairs along a wall. They sat away from the other guests, very close, his arm still around her waist.

"Frankly"—she leaned her head closer to his—"I was just about to make a confession. . . ." She paused to take a steadying breath.

"Oh?" His dark eyebrows rose as he listened intently.

"I can't dance like that." She hooked her thumb in the general direction of the dance floor.

"Oh."

It was all he said, but the simple sound spoke volumes to Kaleene. The slight crinkles around his eyes appeared again as he smiled tenderly at her. Those devastating dimples were back too.

"Well, you'll just have to learn, because I have every

intention of getting you in my arms as much as possible tonight.''

His intense gaze sent little shivers of anticipation up and down her spine. Those shivers pooled against his touch at her waist and vibrated there.

"Will you come outside with me?''

"Of . . . of course.''

The music resonated through the doors outside where several young couples were forming rows in the center of the hay bales. Kaleene watched, fascinated, as they began to do slow stepping and sliding motions in sequence with each other.

"We'll try that first,'' Logan murmured close to her ear as they stopped near the doorway.

They stepped aside as late arrivals made their way in. Two of the people stopped when they recognized Logan.

"How've you been, Logan?'' The tall man in a white cowboy hat thumped Logan's shoulder vigorously.

"Fine, fine. I'd like you to meet Doc's new associate, Dr. Kaleene LeGare.''

"Dr. LeGare,'' the man said heartily as he pumped her offered hand. "We're awfully glad you've chosen our fair community as your new home. Good people and good commerce make a good future, you know. That's what we're all about here.''

"In case you haven't guessed, Mr. Peterson is our mayor,'' Logan said.

The mayor laughed and thumped Logan on the shoulder again. "It shows, does it? Well, my pride in my community is something the citizens will just have to tolerate.''

"It's what we love most about you, dear,'' the serene

woman at his side said. "It's lovely to meet you, Dr. LeGare."

Mrs. Peterson drew Kaleene aside and thoroughly delighted her with a genuine welcome. She chatted for a moment about an upcoming charity auction for the medical center and asked Kaleene if she would be interested in helping on the volunteer committee.

"That sounds like a wonderful cause. I'd love to help in any way that I can," Kaleene said, warmed by the woman's interest in her. As they continued chatting, Kaleene caught snatches of the conversation Logan was having with Mr. Peterson.

When the mayor and his wife moved on inside, Logan drew close to Kaleene again. She studied his profile as he watched the line of dancers for a moment. His posture was relaxed, yet his features seemed just as strong and commanding.

"You know some pretty interesting people in this community," she said, arching a brow at him.

Logan placed his arm around her waist again, smiling as he did so.

"Like"—she eyed him closely—"the mayor, Mr. Lawford, and apparently every business owner in Tumbleweed. Tell me, why is the mayor so interested in your opinion of the town's economic development?"

"I don't know." He smiled as he shrugged his broad shoulders. "Could be because it's almost reelection time soon."

There didn't seem to be a question Logan didn't have a quick answer ready for. Logan seemed just as capable of sharing his opinion on the quality of various lawn fertilizers with George as he was at discussing complex economic issues with wealthy landowners and politicians.

Kaleene pushed her unformed ideas to the back of her mind as more people paused to exchange greetings with Logan and welcome her to the community. She caught sight of Doc for a brief moment, but lost him in seconds as he passed into the barn. Fannie and George waved a greeting across the crowd as they worked their way inside.

The hay bales were fast filling up as people continued to arrive, and Logan brought her over to an empty one. He seated himself straddle-legged over its length and pulled Kaleene down to sit on the corner. Wrapping his arm lightly around her, he pulled her back against him.

"It's called line dancing. Just watch the woman in the red skirt." He breathed the words in her ear. "She's probably the best dancer here. See how she points her toe up when she taps her heel forward?"

Kaleene tried to still her fluttering heart and concentrate on what was happening in front of her instead of what was happening inside her. Logan's moist breath tickled her lobe, making her want to push her body closer to his.

"Now count the steps as you're watching, one, two, three, four. Forward, two, three, back. Turn left, turn right, back, and tap. It's all just combinations of forward, back, side, turn, and tap."

"Yes," Kaleene agreed with surprise. "I can see the individual steps. And it's all about how they put them together?"

"Yes."

He ran his hands down her tingling arms, caressing her sensitive wrists. She felt the gentle pressure of his broad chest against her back with each deep breath he drew. For a while they sat unmoving, letting small talk flow between them.

Later that evening, at the end of one of those lines of dancers, Kaleene and Logan moved back and forth in time to the music. Little of the lantern's glow reached them, and the crowd was sparse here, giving Kaleene an almost euphoric sense of confidence.

Logan kept one arm around her waist, the other on her shoulder, guiding her easily through the steps. He spun her away, holding onto one hand, causing her to turn around until she ended up back in his embrace, hip to hip.

Breathless from the excitement, Kaleene gazed across the inches that separated their lips as they stepped sideways and back. The comforting pressure of Logan's hand was always there, directing her movements. With a rolling crescendo, the song came to an end.

For a moment longer than was necessary, she held on to his arm, wanting, waiting for the perfect moment. He understood her desire. His sensual mouth moved closer to hers. Slightly parting in anticipation, her lips sparked at his first, light touch.

Spirals of giddiness washed through her stomach. Logan's strong arms wrapped around her back and pressed her closer to him. Her knees became weak like tulip stems no longer able to support the blooms that had grown too heavy for them.

Kaleene allowed her body to respond as it was demanding to. She parted her lips as she swayed in his embrace. Distantly she became aware of the music flowing through the night. As Logan slid his hands up to her arms, Kaleene felt surprise as the solidness of a wall touched her back. Logan had deftly moved them from the dance floor to the more discreet shadows at the side of the tall barn.

Aware now of the privacy of darkness that cloaked them, Kaleene ran her hands up to his temples. The hard pulse of his heartbeat drummed against her feathery touch, and she traced its path down his neck into the center of his rippling chest.

Logan responded with fervor, pulling his lips from hers and raining kisses down her cheek to the line of her delicate jaw. He paused and gazed at the dark, seductive outline of her slender neck, arched in response to his caress.

She felt his gaze brush over her and opened her eyes to his astonishingly virile form. Glints of the distant lights shone on his flushed lips, redder now from the burning path they had blazed down her cheek. His eyes, almost as dark as the indigo sky, mirrored the desire in her. Kaleene placed her hand on the side of his face.

Her feeling had grown so fast, too fast. She had to slow the moment down. ''Shouldn't we go back to the party?''

Logan's chest heaved with each breath as he attempted to bring his tumultuous feelings under control. He squeezed his eyes shut, and with an effort finally stepped back from her. A heavy sigh escaped his lips as he glanced back at the people milling about in the glow of the paper lanterns. Soft music drifted from the open doors and faded off into the night sky.

''Good idea, Kaleene.'' He turned back to her and laid a finger softly against her flushed cheek. ''We don't need to go so fast.''

He had read her unspoken fear!

"We have all the time we need to get to know each other. Then we'll see where this takes us, all right?"

Seeking out his hand, she nodded and twined her fingers in his. The sinewy touch of his palm was undeniably magnetic. "Let's start with you showing me what you like to drink." She pointed in the general direction of the party.

"Sure." Logan smiled easily, then gave her a quick kiss on the end of her nose. "We'll do that while I think of what I most want to know about you."

She met the challenging look in his eye with an uplifted chin. At that moment, she felt she wanted to share everything with him. Contented to be at his side, she allowed him to lead her back to the lights and the crowd. They slipped into the flow of people moving inside for food and drinks.

So many new faces and names—Kaleene wondered if every resident of the county was here tonight. Abandoned temporarily by Logan, she stood with a cluster of women, discussing the best time to plant iris bulbs.

"Hey, Clayton," one of the women called as she snagged the arm of a tall man who was circling the room. "You need to meet the new vet." She pulled Kaleene forward and presented her to their host.

Clayton Lawford was a distinguished-looking man, dressed in a dark, western cut suit. A slight graying at his temples gave his aquiline features the aura of a mature but powerful man.

"How do you do, Dr. LeGare?" His voice was strong and deep.

As she returned his greeting, Kaleene found herself speculating about his son. How was Denny getting along with him? She seemed like such a sweet, yet vulnerable girl. It would be terrible if she got her heart broken at such a tender age. But if Clayton's son was anything like his imposing father she had a real challenge facing her.

Clayton moved on through the crowd, and Kaleene scanned the gathering for Logan's dark head. Perhaps he'd decided to check on his little sister before returning. His concern for her was so evident earlier.

Briefly she caught sight of someone on the dance floor wearing a black Stetson hat. Through the press of the crowd, Kaleene couldn't tell if it was Logan. Excusing herself from the women she'd been chatting with, she squeezed through the crowd to the edge of the dance floor. Again she found the familiar-looking black hat, but was still unable to see the owner's face.

The woman he danced with was wearing a very familiar red skirt. Kaleene could clearly see her face. It was the same woman Logan had told her to watch earlier while he was telling her about line dancing.

But this was no line dance. They moved in fast, intricate steps impossible for Kaleene to decipher with her limited experience. A sinking feeling crept over her as she watched the couple move together. The man's hands rested on the woman's curvaceous hips, hers twined around his neck. They moved perfectly in sync with each other's lithe bodies. Kaleene ruefully admitted that they looked perfect together, his height a perfect match for his petite partner, his dark hair a perfect contrast to her fair looks.

The song sighed to an end as the woman pulled her partner's head down. Her lips pursed as she leaned into him and kissed him. As she pulled his head to the side, the shadow cast by the brim of that black hat moved. Kaleene could see his face clearly now. It was Logan.

The sight hit her like a hammer blow. She whirled to flee. Denny stood in her way, as if she had been magically summoned by Kaleene's fleeting thoughts of her a moment ago.

Denny's freckled face was screwed up in a look of barely contained anger. Her hurt eyes flicked from Kaleene to her brother.

"So, he's dumped you for Eva, huh? I thought he would once he found out she was here." Disregarding the sharp gasp that escaped Kaleene's taught lips, Denny continued her hurtful tirade. "Everybody always expected the two of them to get married, you know. They were high school sweethearts, I think."

Kaleene covered her mouth with the back of her hand and dodged around the red-faced girl.

"Anyway, I'm just sorry you had to get hurt by him. . . ."

Kaleene escaped through the crowd, ignoring Denny's fading words.

"—but isn't that what all guys do, hurt the girls who care for them most?"

In the near total darkness along the graveled drive, all the trucks looked alike to Kaleene. She searched up and down for Fannie and George's green Chevrolet, and finally found it when the headlights of a departing car flashed across its side. Quickly she scrambled inside the cab. Exhaustion flooded over her and she leaned back against the cool seat.

Misery surrounded her like a black fog. She closed her

eyes, willing herself not to think about him, concentrating on the music, on the distant sounds of people enjoying themselves. In the dark her breathing became deep and steady.

Uncounted minutes passed before the dome light clicked on, temporarily blinding Kaleene.

"Fannie, looks like we got ourselves a squatter here," George's surprised voice exclaimed. He held the passenger door open.

"Let me see," the curious woman commanded as she shouldered past her husband, "Kaleene, hon. What're you doing here? Where's Logan?"

"I . . . he . . ." She stopped, at a loss for words. Sliding upright, Kaleene levered herself from the truck seat and took a moment to get her thoughts in order. "He's still inside. I wanted to get home early and told him I'd catch a ride with you two. You don't mind, do you?"

"No, of course not," George reassured her. "But it isn't like Logan not to escort a lady home. I don't know what's got into that boy—"

"George." Fannie made a silencing gesture.

"We'd be glad to give you a ride," he said smoothly. After helping his wife into the cab he turned and offered Kaleene a hand.

She gratefully took George's steady hand and slid in beside Fannie. Thankfully they asked no more questions during the drive back home.

Kaleene managed to escape up to her room and shed her clothes on the way to the bathroom. Steaming water rushed into the old tub as she tied her hair up. As the swirling liquid climbed high enough to suit her, Kaleene eased her tired body into it. Slowly the ache inside eased its grip on her heart. She scrubbed her skin with the lavender soap, trying to wash away the heady male scent of Logan from her senses. It lingered despite her best efforts. Tonight, she knew, she would not have a peaceful night's sleep.

That difficult weekend was finally over. The dance was days behind her, three days to be exact, she thought ruefully. This would be her first official day at work, and Kaleene felt determined to make it a good one. She tromped down the stairs, still not used to Fannie's red boots. But she set her heart on looking the part of Doc's competent associate, like a person who belonged in this community. The red boot-tips peaked out from the hem of her jeans.

"You're wearing them!" Fannie exclaimed with delight. She set the stack of plates on the end of the long table and took an appraising look at Kaleene.

"I thought they would get me off to a good start."

"Well, I'm right proud you think so. That sack there," Fannie said, pointing to the hutch near the door, "that's got some walnut muffins in it. You might need a snack today."

Kaleene opened the bag, and the enticing aroma of cinnamon and nutmeg rose up to encircle her head. "Oh, Fannie, how thoughtful of you."

"And there's another message from Logan on the phone table in the parlor."

The third one in as many days. Fannie hadn't added that out loud, but Kaleene heard it in her voice. This one would also go unanswered.

"Thanks, I'll pick it up on my way out."

But she deliberately forgot to. No bad thoughts were going to come with her to work today, she swore as she hurried down the sidewalk in the cool, early morning air. She crossed the deserted highway and reached the front step of the animal clinic just as Dr. Corbin appeared in the doorway.

"Bright and early, I see," he commented as he held the glass door open for her.

"I guess I'm a bit anxious to get off on the right foot."

"Ah, don't you worry any about that. I've seen enough of your work. I know you can do the job." He strolled down the hall to his office, leaving Kaleene to familiarize herself with the place.

Three hours later she was up to her eyes in kittens. Little black kittens, all needle-sharp claws, razor teeth, and spitting mad.

"I found them under the chicken coop."

Kaleene listened attentively to the farmer as he explained what he expected her to do with the little terrors.

"Apparently the mother got killed by something. Could have been a stray dog. Anyway, they've got fleas." He crossed his arms and sat back in the only chair the tiny examination cubicle had.

Kaleene peered into the cardboard box that sat on the exam table between them. "I see." She pursed her lips and nodded her head.

"Well, I can't take them home with fleas." He arched his brows at her.

"Of course not," she hastily agreed.

"The wife wouldn't like it if the girls ended up with fleas just because I thought they could learn a little responsibility. Raising the kittens,'' he added as Kaleene stared blankly at him.

''Oh. Then I'd suggest that after we dip them we clip their little claws. For the girls' protection, you understand.''

''Oh—'' He halted himself before the objection he was obviously forming could reach his lips. ''But they will grow back, right? A farm cat's not much good without claws.''

''Sure. They'll grow back after the girls' have had time to tame the kittens. But I'd recommend your daughters wear thick gloves while handling the kittens for the first few days. Give us a couple of hours and we'll have them ready.''

''Sounds fine.'' As he rose to leave he turned back and eyed her once more. ''I saw you at the Lawford place the other night. You were dancing with my neighbor.'' The farmer smiled approvingly at her, the first look she'd had from him other than a skeptical stare. ''Good man,'' he announced, and donned his hat and left.

Logan. Despite her efforts he had entered her day anyway. She scooped up the box of hissing razor blades and carried them to the wet room. The cardboard box grated across the counter as she slid it back and stood there staring off into space.

How was she ever going to get the sound of his voice out of her mind? When would she lose the feeling of his broad shoulders, his corded arms wrapped securely around her? His kiss—

''Doc LeGare! Phone!'' As usual Velma disdained the use of the intercom system the building was equipped with.

"Who is it?" Kaleene asked as she rounded the corner from the hall to the reception area.

"Your dance partner, Logan." Velma's eyes sparkled as she smacked her gum and wriggled her eyebrows up and down suggestively.

"Please tell him—" Kaleene clamped her lips in a thin line to contain the rest of her outburst. After a moment she continued levelly, "Tell him that I'm very busy and I don't take personal calls during office hours." Icicles dripped from every word.

She turned to make a hasty retreat and brought herself up short, narrowly avoiding crashing into Dr. Corbin. Somehow she managed to dodge around him at the last second and was fleeing down the hall as she heard him swear.

"—worst case of prairie fever I've ever seen."

Chapter Five

"I've been expecting that call for the last few days," Dr. Corbin assured Velma. "Check Kaleene's schedule for me. Is there anything that can't wait until tomorrow?"

"What's going on?" Kaleene asked as she stepped from one of the exam cubicles that bordered the reception area. Her arms were full of a wriggling, energetic Labrador puppy, her first patient of the morning.

Dr. Corbin leaned over the counter and peered through his reading glasses, trying to decipher Velma's handwriting in the appointment book.

"A brood mare," he answered her without taking his attention away from the book.

In the few weeks she'd been working with the man, Kaleene had grown used to his ponderous manner. His curt responses were not a sign of agitation or annoyance, but simply his normal mode of communication.

65

The puppy wriggled more furiously as he caught sight of his master coming through the clinic's front door.

"He's had his shots and is all ready to go," Kaleene said as she handed him to the young woman. "Velma has your paperwork and his new tag. You'll need to get a bigger collar as soon as possible. He's really growing."

"Thanks for taking such good care of my little Sasha," the woman said, more to the dog than to Kaleene. The puppy licked his owner's face as she cuddled him close.

He was such an irresistible sight with his big, drooping ears and impossibly huge feet, just like all Labrador puppies. Kaleene couldn't resist a few more scratches behind his ears before turning her attention back to Dr. Corbin.

"What's this about my schedule?" she asked. This time she had a little more luck penetrating his barrier of concentration. He glanced her way, then resumed his reading.

As Sasha and his owner made their way out the door, Dr. Corbin finally answered her. "We're going to be out for the rest of the day. You,"—he spun the appointment book back around to Velma and thumped his hand on the counter—"call the two appointments she has today and reschedule them for tomorrow. I've got nothing going but paperwork and that can wait for the weekend as far as I'm concerned." He turned to Kaleene and removed his reading glasses. "Well, what are you waiting for? Let's get going!"

As Kaleene hurried to follow Dr. Corbin, Velma waved a message pad at her. "Sam called. Said he was sorry he missed you. Got the days mixed up or something."

Kaleene glanced back and nodded a hasty acknowledgment. It must be someone who missed an appointment, she guessed, and hurried to catch up with the spry, elderly doctor.

"Doc, do you mind me asking where?" Kaleene braced her arm against the window frame of the faded blue Willis jeep. He gunned the engine as he shifted down to a lower gear. They rounded the corner and chugged back up to speed as the town of Tumbleweed shrank behind them.

"Where what girl?"

"Where we're going." She shook her head in amusement, a wry smile stretching across her lips as she watched the wizened older man hunch farther over the big steering wheel.

"Silver Spur Ranch, of course." He spared her a short glance, his bushy eyebrows climbing his creased forehead. "Where were you when Velma told me about the call from the breeding ranch?"

"Dealing with a twenty-pound Sasha."

"Oh." His bluster vanished. "The folks at the Silver Spur, they've got a mare that I've been expecting them to call about. She had trouble last time she foaled."

"Then why did they breed her again?" Kaleene said, a little of the annoyance she felt coloring her tone. One thing she disliked about being a veterinarian was dealing with irresponsible breeders, of any type of animal.

"Not that much trouble." Dr. Corbin tisked at her abruptness. He explained the horse's past minor complication, reassuring Kaleene of the breeder's ethics. "They know what they're doing at the Silver Spur. This horse has a championship title to her name, so they're not going to take any unwarranted risks with her, you can count on that.'' The old Willis bumped roughly as they turned from the smooth highway to a narrower country road.

"Shouldn't be too difficult today. But it'll be a good opportunity for you. It'll let folks around here know you can handle the big critters too.''

Yes, this would be an excellent opportunity. Kaleene knew it was important for the farmers and ranchers to see her out working on large animals with Dr. Corbin.

The people here had relied solely on him for the health care of their animals—livestock and pets—for a long time. Some adjustment would definitely be in order. A show of cooperation and trust between the two veterinarians was essential for the future of their partnership.

"These thin canvas tennis shoes weren't the best choice for today,'' she said, peering down at her feet. Dr. Corbin was wearing brown lace-up work boots, she noticed. He was always prepared.

Of course, one day he would retire. He intended for her to take over his workload eventually. She intended to do everything she could to make that transition as smooth as possible for him as well as the people who lived in and around the tight-knit community of Tumbleweed. She was beginning to care a great deal about this town, developing strong ties with these warm and friendly people.

Growing up here would have been so wonderful. How different things would have been if her father hadn't left his family behind when he fled Chicago. She allowed herself a moment to add to the mental picture she was building of her imaginary childhood spent here. Growing up in a small community like this would have meant having plenty of places to play outside, clean parks, quiet streets, barn dances, Logan.

A tiny knot formed deep in her throat. She swallowed, willing it to fade away. There was no reason to dwell on Logan, she scolded herself. How many days had it been she last saw him? Three days. Almost four. She glanced at her watch—three days and about twenty hours. But who's counting? She shook her head as the old cliché rolled through her mind.

Four days ago she was having lunch in the sandwich shop with Velma. Logan roared by in his shiny blue pickup. Her vision was drawn to him like magic, and the scene burned itself into her mind's eye. His bold profile stood out in the center of the picture while the edges of the truck faded to blue fog.

What had she felt at the time? It was almost a sickening, wrenching feeling, like something vital was being taken from her. That had ended her appetite. Mary couldn't understand her sending back the dessert untouched.

Since that day Kaleene always made a point of sitting with her back to the windows when she had lunch, no matter what restaurant she went to.

"Now, I don't want you getting the jitters," he cautioned. "I expect there'll be a fair amount of eyes on you out here but you just do what you're trained to do. Handle yourself like you've been doing at the clinic and you'll be fine."

"I'm sure I will." She eyed him reproachfully. "You sound more worried than me."

Dr. Corbin chuckled softly, wrinkles deepening around his eyes. "I suppose I might be. But you understand that

Silver Spur Ranch is one of the top quarter horse breeders in the whole country, don't you?''

"No. I wasn't aware of that.''

"And their business pays a big chunk of our bills. They also sponsor the free Dip 'n Stick clinic each summer. Without that, we'd probably have a large population of un-vaccinated dogs and cats in the county.''

"Velma was telling me a bit about the free clinic just yesterday. It takes place in early August sometime, doesn't it?''

"Yes. Over at the coliseum. It's close to the office, and big enough that we can move a lot of animals through in one day. We get help from the Silver Spur hands too. They'll give anybody a lift that calls in. And the Future Farmer kids help out with paperwork and dipping.''

"Is the Silver Spur Ranch the sole sponsor?''

"Yep. And I imagine there'll be quite a few Silver Spur hands around today wanting to see what the new vet can do. Word of mouth from them is the best advertising we could possibly get.''

"Then you needn't worry, Doc. I'll mind my manners and act my most doctorly,'' she chided him.

"I'm sure you will. One more thing though.'' He paused as if deciding the best way to approach the next subject. "Cleopatra is a big quarter horse, seventeen and a half hands tall. If there's any manhandling to be done, you let Logan do it.''

Logan would be there? Her eyes lost their focus on the narrow road that stretched out ahead. Kaleene raised a hand to her flushed face. The heat seemed to lick out at her fingers.

She stared out the side window, trying to bring her thoughts back to some kind of order. With an effort she concentrated on the white rail fence they were passing. The posts flew by like Dr. Corbin's words, unrecognizable from each other.

All the feelings she'd been denying about Logan resurfaced at once. She had to get a grip on her emotions, and quickly. The jeep was slowing, and Kaleene dragged her attention back to the present.

"—pretty good at handling their horses. They usually call me out only for the rarer problems."

They had reached a tall gateway. High above them, the arched entrance bore large metal letters: SILVER SPUR RANCH. A small sign stood beside the gate proclaiming this to be the home of four National Cutting Horse Association world champions. It listed the names of several stallions and offered their stud services.

Lush pastures stretched out on either side of the drive. The green expanse was dotted with powerfully muscled horses whose short coats gleamed in the clear sunlight.

No buildings were in sight from the gate, and Kaleene peered ahead eagerly, her panic and the idea of Logan's presence forgotten. A young filly raced toward the fence. With its tail high in the air, it followed the jeep several yards before turning away to join its dam. Kaleene watched the young horse in pure delight until the jeep dropped over a gentle slope and she lost sight of the young animal. Turning around, Kaleene caught her first glimpse of the ranch house.

"Wow!"

"It is some sight," Dr. Corbin agreed.

Kaleene hadn't realized she had made that comment aloud. As she clapped her hand over her mouth, he laughed.

"I always thought it looked a bit like a southern plantation, myself."

"It's magnificent." She craned her neck back and forth, trying to absorb all of it at once. "Is it two-story or three?"

"Two-story mostly. The Greek columns across the front make it look tall, I suppose. But a lot of the front is the ballroom, and that's open to the roof, just like the entryway is."

"A ballroom?" She couldn't hide the incredulity in her voice. Kaleene stared at the grand structure. Its limestone and brick facade reflected the bright sun off its white surface. Tall, slender windows ran across the front, allowing a great deal of sunlight inside.

"It was built up north someplace. The whole thing was brought here piece by piece more than a hundred years ago." He steered the Willis along the wide road that forked away from the house and turned west down a gentle slope to the cluster of red buildings in the distance.

Several people could be seen working in and around the stables. Some moved bales of hay from a low storage barn to the three stables while other workers were busy tending horses.

Kaleene noticed several foals in the paddocks. There were so many, she marveled, especially this early in the year. But as she stepped from the jeep, the strong Texas sun shining down on her bare head reminded her of how much farther south she was than Indiana. It was later in the breeding season here. This many foals, and so fully developed, were to be expected around here.

She closed the jeep door and stepped to the front to join the elderly veterinarian, who'd pulled his satchel of equipment from the backseat. A glare of sunlight bouncing off the chrome of a metallic blue pickup caught her eye. It was Logan's truck.

"Doc, I want you to know something," Kaleene said softly as she reached a hand out to snag the man's arm. "I'm a competent veterinarian. I can handle a mare as well as your friend the farrier can any day." She quickly released her light touch on his arm and moved off to the front of the middle stable they had parked by. She didn't want to give him a chance to rebuke her.

"Prairie fever," he muttered as he shook his head. "Gets those big city people every time."

Large stalls lined both sides of the airy, well-lit stable. Each stall had solid panels on the lower half, and steel bars on the upper half. Kaleene silently approved of the design that allowed horses to visit with their neighbors. With their natural instinct to herd being so strong, the ability to see other horses nearby would keep them calmer than horses that were stabled in isolation.

She looked at the structure. The four-foot-wide sliding stall doors were white with red trim. The X pattern of reinforcing pipe was red, a reverse of the exterior paint pattern of red walls and white trim that decorated all the stables.

Windows opened to the outside along the sides, and some stalls had exterior doors that led to individual paddocks. The horses in those stalls had free run of their private enclosures.

The benefit of so many open windows and doors made

this the sweetest-smelling stable Kaleene had ever been in. Sunlight, all golden and soft, filtered through the east windows, creating patterns in the air on the floating hay dust as it swirled through the shafts of light.

A scuffling noise from the other end of the barn caught her attention. One of the workers came through the double door at the back end of the extra-wide center aisle. He strode steadily toward them, a bucket gripped in each hand. The sinewy muscles of his forearms bulged under the strain .of the heavy load he carried, and his fingers curled tightly around the handles. Dust brown boots, jeans, and a plaid shirt with the sleeves cut off at the shoulders looked just right on him. There was no hat on his dark hair, nothing to obscure Kaleene's view of his face as he looked up and met her gaze.

Logan strolled toward them, his rolling gait relaxed and easy. A neutral expression defined the clear-cut lines of his face. ''Doc, glad to see you.''

''Well, boy, how've things been going lately?''

''Pretty well.'' Logan set the heavy buckets against a wall. ''Denny's got a new pet she wants to bring in for you to look at.''

''What is it this time?'' His white eyebrows rose higher in alarm.

Logan grinned crookedly before answering. ''An armadillo.''

''Good grief! Where's she keeping it?''

''In a rabbit hutch out by the kitchen door.''

''That girl will be the death of you yet.'' Dr. Corbin turned and surveyed the row of stalls. ''I assume Cleopatra's still in the end stall?''

"All the way down on the left." Logan motioned for them to follow him. "I think it's plenty big enough for us to work in."

For the first time his eyes flicked to Kaleene's face. She saw it starting around his eyes. The tiny crinkles grew, then the dimples appeared. It was a dazzling smile, the kind that could send women's hearts fluttering.

But the fluttering sensation infuriated her. She squelched it as hard as possible. Setting her face in a stern mask, she gazed blandly back.

"You wouldn't mind leaving this to the professionals, would you, Logan?" Dr. Corbin jolted to a stop at her side, but she kept on talking. "Foaling really should be the business of vets and breeders, don't you agree?"

"Uh," Dr. Corbin reached a hand out for her elbow, but dropped it to his side. He arched his brows and tried again, "Kaleene, I thought you'd met Logan before. Velma told me—"

"Of course I've met him before, Doc. You sent him to the bus stop to give me a ride to the Smiths'. That was the day I arrived here from Indiana."

He sputtered in surprise. "Y . . . you mean Sam? The farrier?"

Logan's grin grew wider. His dimples were in full view now, framing his lips perfectly. The gleam in his eyes looked suspiciously like enjoyment. And with the bewilderment Dr. Corbin was voicing, Logan's glee was probably at her expense.

It was time to give this jerk a piece of her mind. She would take his antics at a barn dance, and not cause a scene, but *no one* interfered with her work. No one.

Summoning up her courage, she stepped toe to toe with him.

"Now"—Logan deftly turned away and took Dr. Corbin by his elbow—"How safe a pet is an armadillo?"

She balled her hands into hard fists as the two men walked away. Logan was afraid to face her! There must be some way to handle this situation, without making herself look like an angry—No, she didn't even want to think the words. Jilted woman. Oh! She'd done it anyway!

She stomped past the two men, quickly putting distance between herself and them. As she approached the end stall a soft nickering sound slowed her pace. An almost inaudible murmuring of a human voice accompanied it. Peering through the bars, she saw a man gently stroking a horse's neck.

Kaleene rolled the door open and stepped inside the large stall. What a beautiful sight. She froze and gazed at the sleek, pale chestnut mare who nervously shifted her weight from side to side. Cleopatra's big brown eyes swung around from the man who scratched her nose to regard Kaleene warily. Muscles along her flanks quivered slightly as she snorted.

As she stood still, waiting for the horse to get used to her presence Kaleene surveyed her surroundings. It really was a good-size stall with a bedding of fresh straw, an automatic water system, and a corner hayrack. The grain bucket hung on the corner of the hayrack, its sturdy metal hook smoothly rounded. These horses were indeed well prized by their owner.

A soft impact against her shoulder startled Kaleene back to the realization of why she was here in Cleopatra's stall.

"Sorry." Logan's voice, soft as velvet, brushed across her lobe. "I didn't realize you had stopped in the doorway."

He awkwardly maneuvered around her with Dr. Corbin right on his heels.

"Thanks for staying with her, Jess," Logan said to the man who had been stroking the horse calmly.

Would Logan ever leave her in peace? She'd have to get rid of him somehow, especially if she hoped to concentrate on the job at hand.

"No problem, Boss. Me and Cleo get along real good, even when she don't really want company. Isn't that right, old girl?" he said softly, rubbing the horse's nose one last time. "Ma'am," he greeted Kaleene, tipping his hat as he passed her on the way out of the stall.

"Jess," Logan called to him before he'd gotten more than a foot outside the stall door. "Doc and—" He flicked his eyes at Kaleene.

"Kaleene will do nicely," she informed him and turned to offer a firm hand to Jess.

"Nice to meet you, ma'am." Jess blushed slightly under his deep tan, just enough to warm the tips of his ears.

"They would probably appreciate a couple of chairs," Logan continued. "Just in case we end up spending a lot of time down at this end of the barn."

"Sure thing, Boss. Folding chairs from the tack room be okay?"

What in the world was going on here? Why was Logan ordering this man about? Why was he acting as if he owned the place? As if he was the . . . Realization smacked Kaleene in the face. She turned smoldering eyes on Logan.

Chapter Six

"Boss?" she asked tightly.

"Yes," he agreed.

"Not the local farrier?"

"No," he agreed.

"Owner of the Silver Spur Ranch." So help her, if he gloated right now, she'd, she'd strangle him. She'd wrap her fingers around his scrawny neck and—

"It could be a few hours before we see any action." Dr. Corbin ran his hands along Cleopatra's sides. "You've got her on closed-circuit, I see." He indicated a TV camera mounted high on the wall above the stall.

"Yes. I have monitors in the tack room and in my office up at the house."

House! That wasn't a house. It was a—

"Kaleene."

79

Once again Dr. Corbin's voice shocked her out of her rambling thoughts. She moved carefully to his side.

"I don't think she's as close to delivery as Logan thought she was. Why don't you look her over?"

With slow, assured moved, Kaleene introduced herself to the mare, taking care not to cause her any further stress than she was already under.

"Hello, girl. You're a pretty thing." She patted the silken nose, feeling the horse's warm, gusting breath against her open palm. "Everything will be just fine, now that we're here. Doc and I'll take good care of you and your little foal," she whispered soothingly.

"Thank goodness Velma isn't here. You and I'd be clinging to the rafters about now." She smiled secretly at the thought of the colorful receptionist who had fast become a good friend.

A gleam caught her eye and she turned back just in time to see Dr. Corbin ushering Logan from the stall.

"Right out here will be fine," Dr. Corbin directed Jess as he set down the folding chairs. The white-haired veterinarian placed his bag on one of the chairs and began sorting through it for supplies they might need later.

"I'll check back after a while," Jess said, then left them with Cleopatra.

"She's looking pretty good, Logan. I don't expect she'll need any help from us. But let's wait and see what Kaleene says."

Kaleene couldn't help overhear the two men through the stall bars. Was this a test Dr. Corbin was giving her? He'd made it clear that he wanted her to look competent in front of the Silver Spur employees. But he had just pronounced the horse in perfect condition for this stage of her labor. What else was there for Kaleene to do?

Maybe he felt it necessary to put Cleopatra's owner at ease. After the crazy way Kaleene had acted toward Logan earlier, maybe Dr. Corbin was justified, she chided herself. Regardless, she had a job to do, and she would do it to the best of her ability. Kaleene moved cautiously to the other side of the horse, running her hands down Cleopatra's sides.

Now she could hear a few other workers wandering into this end of the stable. They took up positions, peering through the bars at Kaleene and the mare. This was turning into quite a show. She patted the horse one more time and moved out to join them.

"I'm sure it would be best for Cleopatra if we all left her alone for a while."

"You heard her," Logan said as he waved the workers back. "And it isn't as if you don't get to see enough foaling around this place." He joined the others in a subdued laugh as they moved off to their various jobs. Dr. Corbin and Kaleene followed a few paces behind Logan toward the tack room adjacent to the stable's front entrance.

"Don't you remember sending him to pick me up the day I arrived on the bus?" she hissed to her companion.

"I sent Sam Jordan, the farrier," Doc answered in the same undertone. "He never mentioned missing you."

"In here." Logan stepped aside and ushered them through a door. "We should be able to catch everything from here and still be close enough to be there in a hurry if she needs us." He followed them in and moved to a small desk in the center of the room. After moving books aside, Logan swiveled the desk's closed-circuit monitor around to face the chairs nearby.

"This is marvelous," Kaleene said, trying hard to appear relaxed in the room that seemed crowded with shelves of equipment and supplies. "Did you have this TV system installed just for Cleopatra?"

"She was one of the reasons." Logan turned a dial on a black box mounted on the top of the monitor. A view of another stall popped onto the screen. This one was empty. "That's another stall in this barn. There are three more monitors on the shelves behind you. The other barns are on different circuits. You slide this switch here," Logan said as he demonstrated, "and that gets you a look inside them."

Now the view showed another mare who had obviously just given birth within the last hour or so. The foal was rising to its shaky legs and the mother was licking its damp coat, warming it as she did so.

"A colt." Logan supplied the answer to Kaleene's unvoiced question. His dimples appeared as he mirrored the delight in her eyes.

"He's beautiful. Such a dark bay," she marveled, her eyes fixed on the screen.

"Would you like to go see him?"

"Oh, yes." She sprang to her feet and reached the door in three bouncing strides. Caught up in the excitement of seeing the new foal, she hadn't realized that she didn't know which of the other stables Logan had been showing on the monitor. Turning back to him, she blinked in surprise. He was inches behind her.

"I thought I'd show you where that stall is." He shrugged sheepishly.

"Of course," she answered quickly, and stepped aside to allow him to lead the way.

"Don't mind me," Dr. Corbin called after them. "I'll just amuse myself in here, alone."

"Oh, Doc." Kaleene whipped around and started back through the doorway. "I'm sorry. Logan," she called back over her shoulder. "I really should stay here—"

"Nonsense!" Dr. Corbin scolded her. "You know as well as I do that it could be hours until something happens. Get on along now." He reinforced his order with one of his dire scowls.

Logan tugged gently at the sleeve of her pink shirt. "Better do as he says. Doc's famous in these parts for his bark, but notorious for his bite."

Following Logan out of the stable, she laughed at the ludicrous notion of anyone taking Dr. Corbin's scowl or gruff manner seriously. He was a sweetheart. There was no other way she could think of to describe him.

"The ranch manager oversees the foremen who monitor each barn, and they keep an eye on any mares who are within about a week of foaling." Logan explained the workings of his breeding ranch as they strolled along. He pointed out the different buildings and offices they passed, explaining their function.

Kaleene stretched her stride to match his rolling gate. The tips of her canvas shoes were barely level with his boots as she paced beside him.

"How many mares does the ranch breed in a year?"

"About three hundred."

Logan's casual reply, spoken so plainly, was a surprise. Kaleene's step faltered as her warm brown widened. "Did I hear you right?"

"Yes." A smile played at the corner of his lips.

"This must be the biggest breeding ranch in Texas!" She hurried a few feet to get back in step with Logan.

"Not by a long shot. There's a place down in Elgin that has an operation at least twice the size of the Silver Spur. It's the Southwest Stallion Station. Maybe we'll visit there some time."

"Where's Elgin? In Texas?" Déjà vu washed over Kaleene, bringing a light blush to her cheeks as she remembered asking Logan about where his college was.

"It's down south near Austin. Beautiful country down there. I know you'll like it."

So he wouldn't tease her about the silly question. What a relief. Or had he simply forgotten about her asking whether Texas A & M was in Texas? It was during their drive to the wildlife preserve. She remembered everything about that day.

But goodness! Had he just asked her to take a trip with him? Her head felt as if it were full of fog.

They entered the cool stable, pausing a moment to let a group of men lead several horses out past them.

"We were looking in stall number twenty-seven. That's Shaharazad's stall." Logan waved briefly to the foreman who was in the tack room they passed by.

Two horses nickered to each other from neighboring stalls, and Kaleene stepped to Logan's side as he peered in at them. "What in the world?" she sputtered at the sight of one of the horses. For the past hour she had seen nothing but quarter horses, bays, and chestnuts of all sizes and shades. But this stall held a white horse. And it wasn't all white. There were dark, irregular spots all over its body.

"Denny's gelding," Logan explained. "She wanted something different from what everybody else has." He shook his head in mock dismay.

"Well, she certainly got it," Kaleene marveled.

Logan chuckled in agreement. "I saw him when I was in Colorado on a buying trip. I knew she had to have him."

"He's an Appaloosa, right? A Leopard Appaloosa?"

"That's right, Dr. LeGare."

There was a merry twinkle in his eyes, and suddenly she didn't care whether he was teasing her or not. She simply wanted to see more of that twinkle.

They continued down between the rows of stalls, with Logan slowing his pace enough for Kaleene to peek into each stall they passed. "The trouble is," he continued to explain, "now Denny wants a dalmatian to go with the Appaloosa."

Instantly his words evoked an image in her mind. Denny sat atop the tall, spotted horse, and an equally spotted dog trotted along beside them. "All she would need then would be a polka-dot outfit to complete the look," Kaleene said jokingly.

He laughed with her. His eyes crinkled up around the corners, his dimples popped into sight, and his bright teeth flashed between his parted lips. Kaleene felt herself relaxing inside and began to realize how very strong the magnetism was between them.

"Shaharazad," Logan announced, with a grand flourish

of his hand in the direction of the stall that was now on their left.

The warmth that filled his voice as he spoke about the horse, explaining her lineage and past performances, drew Kaleene's attention to his handsome face, so full of caring and pride in his animals. Her admiration for him grew.

The newborn colt rose shakily to his feet and promptly collapsed forward onto his nose. Shaharazad nuzzled her baby, making sure he was all right. With another burst of strength, he tried again to stand. This time he made it. He bobbed and weaved for a few minutes, then took a lurching step closer to his dam.

"The foreman will mark this down on a log sheet in the tack room. He'll note when the foal begins nursing, and when the afterbirth is expelled."

"So there's a lot of paperwork involved in this type of a job."

Logan nodded ruefully. "Sometimes my foremen tell me they feel more like accountants than ranch hands."

"But where is the foreman for the middle barn?"

"He's off today. Gone to Lubbock with his fiancée to pick out a china pattern. I decided to fill in for him, rather than having one of the others who were off shift work today." Logan stepped away from the stall bars. "I think you met his fiancée. She was at—"

"Boss," Jess called from the end of the stable. "Got a call for you. Line two."

"Thanks, Jess." He raised his voice only enough to be heard by the man whom Kaleene had met earlier in Cleopatra's stall. Logan took Kaleene's arm loosely and strolled back toward the tack room.

As they passed the Leopard Appaloosa's stall, Kaleene glanced in one more time. "What do your folks think of your indulging Denny's whim like that?"

Logan shuffled uneasily and cleared his throat. "I'm raising Denny by myself."

Kaleene arched her brows in surprise. "But I don't understand. She is your sister, isn't she?"

"Yes. Our folks died in a plane crash some years ago. We've been on our own ever since." He took a deep breath and blew it out slowly, then added, "And doing pretty good so far."

"I'm sorry about your loss," Kaleene said and instinctively reached a comforting hand out to his arm. Her fingers felt the rock hardness of his biceps. "I didn't mean to pry, or bring up bad memories."

He stepped closer, into her touch, and her hand slid down his arm. As her fingers neared his hand he captured them in a tender caress. Lightly he traced one finger over the back of her hand. The velvet gentleness of his touch electrified her. She remembered his lips, delivering that earth-moving kiss to hers. Then his lips had worked their way down her jaw, setting her skin on fire with their moist heat. She felt her consciousness sinking into his captivating, midnight blue eyes. Somehow she had to save herself, or be lost forever in their hypnotic depth.

"Logan—"

He didn't allow her to continue. "We should be getting back to Doc." He broke his tenuous hold on her hand. "I'll take the call over there."

The phone call lasted quite awhile. As Logan conducted his business, Kaleene wandered with Dr. Corbin through the stable, trying to calm the butterflies that were flittering around inside her stomach.

They glanced in at Cleopatra, only staying long enough to make sure she was doing just as well as she had been. Things were moving along nicely. The mare was shifting around restlessly, lying down for a moment, then getting up again. This behavior would continue until her membrane ruptured.

The two veterinarians walked slowly up the opposite side of the stable and returned to the tack room when they saw that Logan was no longer on the phone.

"Juanita's bringing over a little lunch from the chow hall. She'll be here in a few minutes," he said from his perch on the edge of the desk. "I don't suppose either of you will mind eating in here?"

In this cramped room with Logan? This day was becoming quite a challenge to Kaleene's oath. She'd vowed never to spend another minute with this man.

"Of course not," Dr. Corbin answered for both of them as he eased into the padded chair he had occupied earlier.

The "little lunch" turned out to be a small feast, in Kaleene's opinion. There were handmade tamales and tortillas, along with cheese, refried beans, and Spanish rice. For dessert, Juanita brought a large platter of empanadas, a folded pastry filled with a cooked pumpkin mixture. They were warm and delicious. They also helped put out the fire in Kaleene's mouth that the tamales had started.

"That was unbelievable," she said as she sagged back in her chair. "Are all of Juanita's meals like that?"

"Yep!" Logan's midnight blue eyes twinkled at her.

"My dad always told me, you feed a hand right, he'll earn his pay."

"I think that's 'treat a man right.' But you won't get any complaints from me," Kaleene informed him hastily, throwing her hands up in surrender as Logan held a half full platter of empanadas out to her.

"Juanita's a great cook. She oversees things at the chow hall, but spends most of her time up at the house. She's taken care of things since Denny and I have been on our own. I honestly don't know what I would have done these past few years without her."

Kaleene leaned back in her chair, finding it easy to relax as she listened to Logan and Dr. Corbin talk about their lives here in this wide-open country. She occasionally stopped them with a question, but mostly just listened. The afternoon hours passed easily.

"Hey, we're finally getting this show on the road, folks," Dr. Corbin happily declared as he pointed to the TV monitor that sat on the desk amid an assortment of dishes and silverware.

Cleopatra's water had broken. Allantoic fluid dripped to the straw bedding beneath her as the mare paced around a few steps. Suddenly she lay down in the center of the stall. Although there was no sound accompanying the picture, they could see by the flair of her nostrils that the mare was grunting loudly now.

The contraction eased and Cleopatra's legs relaxed for a moment. Kaleene could see the sheen that the mare's sweat had added to her smooth chestnut coat. This was so exciting, much more so than the few foalings she had attended at college. There, she had been too intent on clinical observations to really enjoy the breathtaking experience of watching a new life enter the world.

Anticipation scooted Kaleene to the front edge of her seat. Logan leaned closer to the monitor also, just over her shoulder. She kept her eyes glued to the screen, watching Cleopatra's breath puff in and out, but it was Logan's breath she felt tickling the back of her neck.

Once again the mare strained under the urging of another contraction, her legs stretched out straight from her body. "We'd better see something pretty soon, Cleo," Dr. Corbin said softly to the image on the screen.

Nervous minutes ticked by as they all waited.

"Time's up," Dr. Corbin declared as he pushed himself up from his chair.

As the white-haired man hurried down the wide aisle to Cleopatra's stall Kaleene was close on his heels. He stooped to pull supplies from his satchel, which rested on the chair closest to the stall door.

Kaleene peered through the bars as she waited for him. Hooves! She could see tiny hooves covered in a whitish membrane protruding from under Cleopatra's long tail.

"Doc," she called in a harsh undertone. Waving frantically in his direction with her head still pressed against the bars, she accidentally struck his shoulder. "Sorry," she whispered breathlessly as she gripped the older man's shirt and hauled him to the bars beside her.

"The foal's coming out," she said in the same hushed but urgent voice. Then a nose followed the two front hooves. Kaleene turned her gleaming eyes to her companion.

She jumped an inch despite herself, then instantly released her grip on the man's shirt. It wasn't Dr. Corbin she had hauled up to the bars. Somehow, it had been Logan's pearl-snapped shirt she had twined her fingers in. Logan's dark blue eyes stared back at her.

It's his mesmerizing eyes, she thought. *That's what makes such an impact. That's what drives all coherent thoughts away.*

Deploring her weakness for the sight of him, Kaleene directed her attention back into the stall. Dr. Corbin moved up on her other side, and she glanced his way. "The foal isn't kicking clear of the mare. Should we go in now?"

"A couple more moments won't hurt," he replied. But soon they moved slowly into the stall. The mare snorted nervously at their presence. Kaleene knelt by her tail, and Dr. Corbin joined her. Together they worked to ease the foal out. After the shoulders emerged, the rest of the body quickly slipped free.

The two doctors backed away, giving Cleopatra a chance to take over the care of her newborn foal. She stretched her head around and nuzzled the wet sack. The membrane broke at the outstretched front hooves and began inching back over the foal's body, revealing first its big nose, then its whole head.

Cleopatra turned away and laid her head down on the soft straw, obviously too exhausted to do anything further. The two doctors returned to the still foal.

Kaleene stripped the membrane off the moisture-slick body as Dr. Corbin carefully cleared the tracheal passage and verified a steady heartbeat. Kaleene rubbed and thumped the rib cage, hoping to get the foal to breathe without further intervention on the part of the humans.

"Do you want to do mouth-to-mouth?" she asked.

Dr. Corbin rocked back on his heels before asking, "Have you ever done it on a foal?"

"Yes. While I was in college I assisted at a foaling that went something like this one is going."

"Okay then." Dr. Corbin nodded. "It's your call, so it's your job."

"Me and my big mouth," she said, and grinned at him.

"And just in case we need something more, I'll get that syringe I prepared earlier."

Kaleene concentrated on blowing big breaths into the still form between her knees. She adjusted her hold on the slippery body and tuned out her surroundings. The strong heartbeat pulsed under her fingers, and the moist heat of the foal rose up, bringing the pungent smell of birth fluids with it.

Subconsciously she noted it was a filly. The damp coat was a light chestnut, just like her dam's. She would be a beautiful horse, if only they could get her to breathe! Seconds ticked by as Kaleene worked, but it seemed more like hours. Again she pulled her mouth from the filly's nose, and this time a warm whiff of air blew strongly back at her.

"She's breathing!" Kaleene exclaimed in delight. The filly gave an energetic wriggle of her almost one hundred pounds, breaking the umbilical cord and rocking Kaleene back against the strong arms that were ready to catch her.

As the filly slid from her loosened grasp, Kaleene looked up into Logan's dimpled face. Sometime during her struggle to save the filly's life, Logan had entered the stall. He had knelt quietly behind her, ready to lend support if she needed it.

Cleopatra was recovering her strength and now took a renewed interest in her baby. She craned her long neck back and began licking at the filly. In a few moments she rose to her feet and attacked her task more vigorously.

"She's so beautiful," Kaleene whispered in awe.

"She sure is," Jess murmured in quiet agreement.

Kaleene glanced up at the source of that unexpected voice from her ungraceful position halfway in Logan's lap and halfway crouching in the soft straw bedding. A sea of faces peered back through the stall's bars at her.

Apparently every worker who could get away from their task for a few minutes had come to see the excitement. Smiles decorated the faces that pressed up against the cool steel. Delight in the happy outcome was evident everywhere.

Logan shifted his supporting grip on Kaleene, sliding his strong fingers down from her shoulders and cupping her elbows. He was down on one knee. Deftly he shifted her to a sitting position on his raised knee, leaving his hands where they were for the moment. A small tremor started in her fingertips and worked its way along her arms to the bare flesh Logan was caressing.

His fingers began making tiny, massaging circles around her elbows. The flesh was becoming more sensitive with each passing moment. As one of his hands abandoned its tiny stroking motions and left her arm she instantly regretted the loss, then had to hold in a gasp as he brought his hand to rest on her waist.

His chest heaved against her back as he cleared his throat

with the smallest of sounds. Could he be as shaken by their contact as she?

"I . . . " He paused to clear his throat again. "I guess we should leave mother and daughter alone for a while," he admitted, his voice barely above a whisper.

Kaleene recognized the strained tone in his voice as his warm breath brushed her reddened cheek. She nodded her head in agreement and felt his fingers tighten for a moment. He must be reluctant to break the physical contact they shared. She found herself liking the idea that—unlike the night at the barn dance—this time it was Logan who had to move away, to break the tension building between them.

This time it was he who had to clear his throat and suggest they move back into the crowd of people. Last time, she could see in his eyes that he knew the effect his touch had on her. Now the tables were turned.

Chapter Seven

As gracefully as possible, she rose from his knee. Still she was shocked at the break of contact with him despite being braced for it. Apprehensive of upsetting Cleopatra, Kaleene moved slowly to the stall door, checking her startled reaction as it rolled open at her approach. One of the faces must have been watching Logan and her. One or more, she amended her thought. Just exactly how many, she didn't want to know.

"Good job, Doctor," Dr. Corbin said as she emerged from the stall with Logan a step behind her. The formality he exhibited was for the benefit of the Silver Spur hands gathered around them, she knew. He had said this would be like free advertising. The word of these men and women would be the best endorsement she could hope for.

Logan stepped to Dr. Corbin's side and offered his hand to her as well. As their palms made contact a brief grimace

95

flicked across his ruggedly handsome face. Kaleene's brows shot up at his reaction, then the sensation registered on her as well. Logan slid his fingers from hers and glanced at the slippery mess covering her hands and forearms. Cleopatra's filly had managed to make a pretty good mess of Kaleene's exposed flesh.

Pulling a cloth from his equipment bag, Dr. Corbin began wiping his right hand, grinning at her deplorable state as he did so.

"It's all part of the job," she reminded him, completely aware of Logan wiping his hand futilely against the thigh of his jeans.

"Maybe we had better go up to the house and clean up a bit," Logan suggested.

"But I should stay here," she protested. "The afterbirth hasn't been expelled yet, and someone should keep an eye on Cleopatra until that happens. We don't want to risk her developing septicemia. If the afterbirth isn't all out soon—"

"Beth," Logan interrupted Kaleene, indicating a robust-looking woman with ruddy cheeks, "will be keeping an eye on Cleopatra."

"But aren't you—"

"My shift's over. It's five o'clock," Logan explained. "Beth's shift is from now until two in the morning."

Beth nodded and made shooing motions with her deeply tanned hands. "Now, why don't you people get out of here and let me get on with my job? Paperwork is piling up by the minute," she added good-naturedly. "That goes for all you gawkers too." She waved enthusiastically at the small crowd still milling around Cleopatra's stall.

Everyone, including Kaleene, took a last look at the newest addition to the Silver Spur. The filly was finally on her shaky legs getting her fill of the colostrum that Cleopatra was producing. This first milk would soon be replaced with mare's milk, after the filly received important antibiotics from her mother. It was a gift from nature, Kaleene marveled, a gift that nature shared among humans and horses alike.

Dr. Corbin finished packing his bag, then the three of them moved from the warm stable outside into the refreshing west Texas breeze. As they approached the faded blue Willis, Kaleene stopped.

"Doc, I can't ride in your jeep like this," she exclaimed, staring down at her shiny, slippery arms and sodden clothes. A stray piece of straw chose that moment to fall from her honey-colored hair.

"You can ride in my truck," Logan offered.

The hopeful expression on his face bewildered her at first. Did he hope she would refuse? That wouldn't explain the feeling she had that his look of hope was mixed with genuine desire. But what man would want a slimy, gooey woman dirtying up his upholstery? The idea was absurd.

Her disbelief was easy for Logan to see. "I have a blanket I'll spread over the seat," he informed her, stalling any objections she might raise before she could possibly voice them.

She sat stiffly beside him during the short ride from the stables to Logan's home. This was getting to be intolerable. She had spent almost the entire day with him, totally destroying her oath to stay far away from him.

And her hope of keeping that oath in the future? Kaleene looked around at the impressive buildings they passed, the spacious bunkhouses, the row of small cottages. Now she realized it would probably be impossible for her to stay in Tumbleweed and avoid contact with Logan.

His prominence in the community was evident. She had wondered why everyone she met seemed to know Logan, and know she had gone to the barn dance at the Lawford home with him.

This was rapidly turning into an impossible situation. The interference with her work would be too difficult to get around. But the feeling of defeat that was overcoming her was the thought that she had come here searching for information about her father. These churning feelings for Logan were getting in the way of that goal.

Would she have to abandon her search and leave town? No! The thought of giving up was too painful to contemplate. She glanced at Logan. She couldn't get rid of the image of his lips pressed against that other woman's willing mouth.

A blush darkened her cheeks as she remembered the hurt and humiliation it had caused her that night. Denny's comments had added to the pain, Kaleene recalled. Was this how her mother had felt when her father had left them so long ago in that Chicago suburb?

For the first time, Kaleene realized she had always feared her father had left for another woman. That wasn't what her mother had told her, but Kaleene grew up with the fear deep inside that he'd moved on to start a new family.

Could that fear be the reason she'd never had a serious relationship with any boy when she was growing up? Her mother always said she was studying too hard to pay much attention to boys . . . But was that the real reason? Kaleene shook her head, doubt rolling through her heart. She had always feared being rejected, abandoned. What better way to avoid that danger than to never allow anyone the chance to do so?

Logan glanced from the road to Kaleene, and she quickly averted her eyes from his virile form.

Slow, careful breaths helped her steady her quaking nerves as he approached the tall house. A winding lane led from the main road down the few yards to the low brick fence that surrounded the impressive structure. She eyed the windows and round turrets set at the corners of the house.

"This is definitely a house someone could get lost in."

"I suppose so," Logan said lightly, a crooked smile accompanying his words.

Kaleene blushed again, and it irritated her. She hadn't meant to speak aloud. She simmered as Logan drove along the brick drive to the grand front entrance with its wide, stone steps. Dr. Corbin parked his jeep behind them as Logan helped Kaleene from the truck. He ushered his guests up the steps and across the deep portico that bordered the house on three sides.

How relaxing it would be to sit out here in the cool evening breeze and watch the brilliant Texas sunsets. Kaleene could see herself perched on the wooden swing with Logan, sipping iced tea. She could see that all too easily, she ruefully told herself.

The front door, with its leaded glass inset, wasn't locked. He swept it wide for her and Dr. Corbin as they followed him into the vaulted entryway. The bare hardwood floor gleamed in the glow of the late-day sun that streamed through the glass as Logan closed the door. It was more of a wide hallway—she'd been in Chicago tenements smaller than this—with several doors leading from it, and a curved stairway at the other end.

"Juanita! Sara!" Logan called. "We have company."

"Beth phoned me with the news, Mr. Beckett." A lovely, soft-spoken woman met them in the living room as Logan led them through the house.

Kaleene tried to take in the sight of the place all at once. The silk *lampas* wall covering and the decorative plaster work of the ceiling spoke eloquently of another era of grace and sophistication.

But the most amazing thing of all was how well Logan fit into his surroundings. He was very much the master of his domain. He dropped his key ring in a dish on the oak harvest table. His black Stetson hat went flying toward a marble buffet and managed to slide to a stop before falling off the end.

"This is Kaleene LeGare," Logan said to begin formal introductions. "Kaleene, this is Sara, my housekeeper. She helps Juanita keep things running around here." His affection for the woman showed in his easy manner.

Does he also kiss her on dance floors? Kaleene couldn't stop the idea from taking shape in her head. The thought sent a stab of pain through her heart.

"I'm glad to meet you." Sara held out her hand. "I've heard a great deal about you."

Kaleene struggled to appear calm and, like Dr. Corbin wanted, the competent professional. She held her sticky, yet drying hand out, then pulled it back in dismay when she realized she was about to contaminate yet another person. "Maybe I should wash first." She tried to put a friendly smile on her face, but wasn't sure how successful she was.

Sara laughed, understanding Kaleene's physical discomfort, then promptly relieved her mental angst as well. "I believe you met my husband down at the stables—"

"Sara!" a plaintive call came from the curved stairway in the hall they had just passed through. "We need you really bad."

Denny's voice, Kaleene finally identified it. The call was followed by many shuffling sounds, too many for one teenager to have made.

"They're getting ready to go to Plainview," Sara informed Logan when he arched a questioning brow her way. "Denny's slumber party," she added when he still seemed just as confused. "Juanita has gone to her sister's anniversary celebration in Amarillo, you remember her making the plans, I'm sure. Jess and I are driving the girls to Plainview for a burger and a movie. We should be back a little after midnight."

"Oh. I completely forgot," Logan said with a groan.

"They'll be leaving in about twenty minutes. If you don't mind waiting for—"

"Sara!" This time the call sounded more panicked.

"Go ahead." Logan waved at the housekeeper. "I'll take care of our grown guests. Doc, you know where the washroom is, the one by the kitchen, don't you?"

The older man muttered something about not being completely senile. He made his way from the room through the door Sara had appeared from.

Logan turned his attention back to Kaleene. She felt his

eyes slide appraisingly up her body, pausing when they finally reached her face. He seemed to be regarding her flushed lips, which at the moment were none too clean.

"I don't think any of the washrooms downstairs will be adequate for your needs. There's one bathroom upstairs that should be teenager-free."

Logan led her back through the double-pocket doorway down the long hall in the direction Sara had taken. They ascended the curved stairway, their footsteps muffled in the deep Persian rug that was held in place with brass bars across the back of each step. At the top landing Logan turned left, away from the giggles and occasional shrieks that drifted from the various bedrooms to the right.

Another rug of the same dark red Persian design ran the length of the upper hall. Paneling covered the lower half of the wall and more of the silk *lampas* covered the upper half. They walked in silence past credenzas, marble tables, and floor lamps to the last door on the left. Eager to get the stickiness off her hands and arms, Kaleene followed closely behind Logan through the massive door.

The room was masculine in every aspect. Heavy black walnut furniture, pieces that must have been well over a century old, looked diminutive in the spacious room. Thick brocade curtains covered the long, west-facing windows and the canopied bed. A curved couch and two chairs sat near a fireplace on the north wall. How cozy and inviting this room must be on those long Texas winter nights. That big bed with its pile of pillows would be so wonderful to sink into.

"Ahem." Logan cleared his throat noisily.

Kaleene whirled around, embarrassment flushing her

grimy cheeks. She shouldn't be invading his privacy like this. He had caught her gawking, and it didn't make her feel good at all.

The silence of the room roared in her ears. She could no longer hear the girls down the hall, and her eyes slid to the closed door. Could things get much more uncomfortable for her? Probably not.

"It's through there." Logan pointed at one of the doors opposite the fireplace.

She followed him inside the tiled room. It to reflected the masculinity if its occupant. Dark reds and greens were everywhere. The floor was the same hardwood she had seen throughout the house. The round window, with its etched glass, was covered with a sheer curtain. A soft, dark green rug covered the floor in front of the deep tub that she eyed longingly. A quick scrub of her arms and hands, then a little dabbing at her clothes was all Kaleene had intended to do.

But then she caught sight of herself in the mirrored wall. Her hair was still full of bits of straw. Gray streaks ran down her face and disappeared into the neck of her shirt. And the shirt—Kaleene eyed it with disgust. She didn't need to look at her jeans, she could feel the clammy wetness of them against her thighs. She needed a shower, and a long one.

"There's shampoo in here, use whatever you like," Logan said as he opened a cabinet to reveal an array of bottles and jars. "Towels are in here." He pointed behind her and she stepped sideways to avoid brushing against him. "I'll rustle you up something else to wear while you're showering," he offered.

"Oh, that would be wonderful." She tried not to sigh in relief at the thought of changing out of her soiled clothing.

"All right." He moved by her back to the door and paused with his hand on the glass knob. "Anything else I can get you?"

His eyes seemed to bore right into her, seeking out her inner thoughts and desires. "N . . . nothing, thanks," she stammered. *Just go before I make a fool of myself,* she silently pleaded.

He gave her a long look at his dimples, then pulled the door shut. Kaleene stood riveted to the spot for a moment, unable to organize her thoughts. Slowly she turned and surveyed the room again. It smelled of soap. Logan's soap. She closed her eyes and inhaled the heady scent of him. A mixture of exotic spices, but undercut with her own scent, which, at the moment, wasn't very pleasant.

Quickly she unbuttoned her shirt and peeled it off. She tossed it into one of the marble sinks of the double vanity and shucked her jeans and underwear. They went into the sink on top of the shirt. What should she do with them? Glancing around, she spotted a wastebasket. There was nothing in it but a disposable plastic liner. She removed the liner and transferred her clothes to it. After a moment's hesitation, she added her socks and damp shoes too then tied the top of the bag closed.

There! Things were starting to smell better in here already. After a liberal use of Logan's mouthwash, she started to feel human again. Soon the room was steamy and Kaleene gloriously scrubbed her skin under the hard spray. She shampooed her hair three times.

Stepping from the tub wrapped in a fluffy bath sheet,

Kaleene stood in front of the mirror and combed her damp hair. The weight of the water straightened its natural curls so much, the dark strands almost reached her waist.

How very much like her mother's her hair looked when wet. Kaleene was suddenly struck with the similarity between her face and her vivid memory of her mother's. But the face in the mirror had none of the worried, wary look her mother had always had. Not always, she corrected herself. That look wasn't there in the wedding picture she had of her parents. Those extra lines, the downward drawn mouth came after Kaleene's father left them.

Turning her back on the mirror, Kaleene wondered what she should do now. Logan had promised to find her some clothes to wear, but where was he now?

Hanging on a hook she saw a dark robe. It had a paisley pattern, obviously Logan's. Kaleene shrugged out of the soft towel and pulled the robe on. It held a trace of his scent as well as spices and Texas sunshine.

She peeked through the bathroom door. It was empty, so she padded barefoot toward the hall door but a flash of white on the bed caught her eye before she made it. A man's white shirt, a pair of jeans, much too small for Logan, and thick socks. No underwear, she realized as she pulled the socks on her cold feet.

Hastily she pulled on the jeans and buttoned the fly closed. Almost a perfect fit. Whose could they be? Not Denny's—they'd be inches shorter. She scooped up the shirt and dashed back to the bathroom. Throwing off the robe, she jerked the shirt on. After tucking it in she noted that the jeans fit better.

Quickly she tidied the bathroom and picked up the plas-

tic bag of clothes on her way out. Ready to face the day—
or rather, ready to face Logan—Kaleene made her way out
and down the stairs.

The house was silent. Sara must have already left with
Denny and her guests. She would now be alone with Logan
if Dr. Corbin weren't here. Thankfully, she reflected, he
was just down these stairs.

"Hi."

Logan stared boldly up at her from the bottom step. The
jet black waves of his hair curled softly about his rugged
features, creating a striking contrast of light and dark. Kaleene seemed to float down the stairs, her shoeless feet
making no sound at all. Logan waited for her, his blue eyes
drilling into her, making her pause a few steps above him.

"I feel much better now." She searched for something
more significant to say. "Your bedroom is beautiful." That
wasn't it, she admonished herself. And beautiful was definitely not the right word to describe that den of masculinity.

"Handsome," she quickly amended, then wished she
hadn't. "Nice," she declared. "Your bedroom is nice."
Daring him with her eyes to say anything but 'thank you,'
Kaleene joined him on the bottom step.

"Thanks," he replied levelly.

But somehow, Kaleene heard a deeper message in his
seductive tone.

"I thought we'd have dinner while we're waiting for you
to declare Cleopatra in the clear."

"Has she passed the afterbirth?" Kaleene was instantly
the professional.

"I just spoke to Beth on the phone in my office. Nothing yet, but we still have two hours before the deadline."

"Can I take a look at Cleopatra on your monitor?"

"Sure. My office is right through here."

He ushered her into a library and through another doorway. This room was paneled in deep reddish oak, and well isolated from the rest of the house. On a wall of deep shelves she saw several monitors; Logan activated one, bringing Cleopatra's stall into view.

Kaleene was enraptured by the sight of the young filly at her mother's side. It was hard to believe that she had held that young life in her hands less than an hour ago.

"Incredible," she murmured.

"Yes," Logan tenderly agreed.

They stood shoulder to shoulder, gazing at the screen, lost in their thoughts at the miracle they had witnessed and been a small part of that day. Neither moved until mother and daughter stepped to a corner of the stall that the camera didn't cover well.

Sighing, purely from contentment, Kaleene turned from the monitor and crossed the room to the windows that looked out along the back of the house. In the distance, she could see the tops of the red stables. The other buildings were out of sight behind the rolling landscape.

"Feeling hungry yet?" Logan had slipped up beside her.

"I guess so," she was surprised to admit.

"Oh, I forgot to mention earlier. Doc left some medications and supplies in the entry hall for you."

"Left them? I don't understand."

"I mean, before he went back to town. He left whatever

he thought you might need for Cleopatra, just in case she doesn't meet the deadline for passing the afterbirth.''

"Doc went back to town?'' She sounded like a parrot, repeating Logan like that. She had to stop it, and right now. But had she heard him right? Had Dr. Corbin left her here?

"He got an emergency call from Velma while you were in the shower. Something about a sheep and a porcupine.''

Logan turned his gaze back to the window. Kaleene took a deep breath and did the same thing.

"I told him I'd give you a ride home when you were done here.''

She was alone with Logan. Completely alone. They stood side by side, gazing silently at the darkening landscape.

Chapter Eight

"So you've raised Denny on your own since college?"

"Actually she was with me at college for the last two months before I graduated. I couldn't leave her here with hired help, she was lost enough as it was after our parents were killed in that plane crash." Logan moved skillfully about the kitchen as he poured the soufflé mixture in the porcelain dishes and placed them in the oven.

Sitting at the table, Kaleene watched Logan's assured movements with admiration as he prepared their dinner. Idly she munched on the remains of her Caesar salad, waiting for him to continue his story. How effortlessly they settled in to the evening's routine of sharing their histories, she marveled. Logan was such an easy man to talk to, so charming and open. But she'd managed to steer clear of her family history all evening, concentrating instead on her

109

love of animals and her work. She listened intently as Logan shared his life's twists and turns.

"And wasn't that a pleasant experience." He loaded his voice with sarcasm as he continued once the oven door was closed. "That was before Juanita joined us. The housekeeper we had then wasn't very accommodating, but I brought her and Denny back to A & M with me. We were all crammed into my apartment, until the day I graduated." He sat down opposite Kaleene and took a bite of his salad.

"What about the rest of Denny's school year?"

"She was in third grade at the time. The principal knew how traumatized she was, so he gave us lesson plans and let us take her schoolbooks with us. She and I studied together each evening and they tested her when we got back home."

"It must have helped her to see you going on with your life." Kaleene felt her heart squeeze in her chest. The thought of Denny orphaned at such a tender age and Logan saddled with the responsibility of helping the little girl through her grief while he was suffering too . . . It was hard to understand why people had to go through such things.

"I think it did help her to be with me, both of us working together. I know having her at my side helped me. Of course there have been times in the past few years that I can honestly say it's been a real trial." He listed several of Denny's surprise pets she'd collected from the wild over the years.

A buzzer interrupted them and Logan hurried to remove the Parmesan soufflés. All conversation stopped as they concentrated on the delicious flavors of the hot food.

It was an incredible meal, the only way to end an incredible day. "Thanks for dinner. You're a marvelous cook," Kaleene complimented Logan as she helped carry dishes to the kitchen sink.

"You sound surprised." He allowed his dimples to deepen in his cheeks.

So they were back to verbal sparring again. Kaleene didn't think she could play that game much longer tonight. It was rapidly getting dark outside the kitchen window and her body was telling her that she had already had too long of a day.

"I think I should check on Cleopatra. The deadline is in about fifteen minutes."

"I did that while you were washing your hands for dinner. Everything's fine now," Logan said as he tidied the counter.

"What?" Kaleene froze with her eyes locked on him. "You got that news and didn't tell me?"

Logan stopped wiping the counter and turned to Kaleene. "Beth said everything went according to the book. I don't see what the problem is."

"You don't—" She snapped her mouth shut and stared wide-eyed at him. With an effort, she unclenched her hands and tried to will the flush from her face.

"Logan, I'll explain it to you someday. Now"—she worked hard at keeping her voice level—"maybe you could give me a ride home?"

The twin porch lights of the bed-and-breakfast shone softly through the dark night.

"Thanks again for the use of the clothes," Kaleene said, pulling her bag of soiled things from the floor of Logan's blue truck as he parked against the curb. He switched off the engine and she felt an uneasy, thick silence fill the cab. "I'll send these back as soon as I can." She fumbled in the almost total dark for the door handle.

"Kaleene," he said in an urgent hush. "I just wanted to make sure you would stay for dinner."

She turned, searching the darkness for his eyes.

"I'm sorry I didn't tell you that I phoned Beth."

In the deep shadow she could hear his breathing. She knew where he was, but couldn't see his face. But she didn't really need to. She knew every line, every plane, and his voice held his emotions clear enough for her to understand them.

"It's just . . . well, you're probably going to think this is trite, but"—Logan paused again, bracing himself—"I've never really known a woman like you."

He was right. It was trite. Kaleene felt her back stiffen.

"You're so serious, so businesslike." Logan felt his words were getting worse by the minute, as if he was galloping headlong to the edge of a cliff and still couldn't stop.

Serious? Businesslike? Of course she was. All her life she'd had to be. Probably a total opposite of Eva. The hateful name jangled in her mind.

"I wanted a chance to ask you why you left the barn dance without me. I was hoping you would give us another chance, maybe we could see each other. . . ."

So he wanted to see her. And how many other women at the same time?

"I don't think so, Logan. I don't think I'm right for you," she stated flatly. Her fingers finally hooked around the door handle and she jerked on it with her last word.

She fled the truck and dashed up the walk to the bright pools of light on the porch.

Thankfully George was still awake, and opened the door for her so she didn't have to search the pockets of her soiled jeans for a key. Kaleene bolted up the stairs as she threw a hasty good-night parting to George.

Horrible dreams filled her long night. Logan kept wandering in and out of the animal clinic, bringing different women with him each time. Tears were running down her cheeks, and Dr. Corbin kept insisting that if she would get a dalmatian puppy everything would be all right.

Kaleene woke tangled in the bed linens and completely exhausted. The room was bright with the early morning sun, and she rolled over to glare accusingly at the alarm clock on her bedside table. Six o'clock. A ray of sunshine peeked above one of the willow branches outside her window and stabbed her in the eye. She jerked upright, then sank back against the headboard. Her temples pounded. Rolling out of bed, she went in search of an aspirin.

With a glass of water and the pill bottle in her hand, Kaleene sank back on the side of the bed. Beside her on the table was her parent's wedding picture, its silver frame glinting in the sunlight. It was time to get more serious about finding that farm. Starting this afternoon, she swore.

Regrettably, the morning at the clinic was slow. She treated a cat for a minor scrape, looked through piles of fashion magazines with Velma, and straightened her desk for the hundredth time. Finally Velma called to her and suggested they go to lunch. Kaleene hurried from her office as voices came from the waiting area.

"No, you can't peek." A woman's scolding tone drifted throughout the doorway.

"Oh, come on. One little peeky-weeky won't hurt nothing," Velma wheedled.

"The card's sealed, now leave it alone."

"Well, you could at least tell me who sent them," Velma insisted.

"Forget it, Vel."

Kaleene stepped around the corner and saw a young woman holding a glass vase full of white roses. They were stunningly arranged in a spray surrounded by tiny buds of baby's breath. Silver-green leaves trailed down the vase's sides. A small envelope hung from a white ribbon among the leaves.

"Dr. LeGare?"

"Of course that's her," Velma scoffed. "Didn't you meet her at the sandwich shop last week?" Velma turned her impish grin on Kaleene. "They're for you, Doc LeGare. Go ahead, open the card. Let's see who they're from."

Kaleene took the vase and murmured a thank you as the young woman left.

"That must be every white rose they had in the shop," Velma decreed.

"They're lovely. . . ." Kaleene felt overwhelmed at the size of the arrangement.

"Of course they are. Now open the card and tell me who they're from!"

Kaleene looked for a place to set the vase, and watched with arched brows as Velma swept fliers and pamphlets from the counter to her desk in an untidy pile. Carefully she set the heavy vase down in the cleared spot and slipped the envelope from its clip.

With trepidation she pulled the embossed card out. Scrawled across the middle were two words: "I'm sorry." Her eyes caught on the masterful strokes of the bold signature.

A tight, itching feeling formed at the back of her throat. Kaleene traced her finger over the raised design and slid her nail down the side of the card. This was no 'phoned-in' order. That was undoubtedly his signature. She slid the card back in the envelope.

"Well?" Velma demanded.

"Logan Beckett." Kaleene spoke his name softly, but still felt a jarring sensation from the sound of it. A watery blur obscured her vision and she hastily reached up to wipe her eyes.

"Oh." Velma sighed.

Without a word, Kaleene took the roses back to her office. There, no one else would see them and ask her any questions.

Their lunch chatter was subdued at first. Today Velma chose a Mexican restaurant where she swore the food was truly authentic. She promised that the sauce that was supposed to be mild really would be mild, and the sauce that was supposed to be hot would burn a blister on your tongue. Kaleene tried to smile at the colorful language Velma used.

Velma steered the conversation in all directions at once, working hard to avoid any mention of Logan, and they made it through the meal with only little stretches of awkward silence.

The clinic was busy the rest of the afternoon; Kaleene avoided her office until closing time. She stood in the doorway of the cramped room, stunned anew by the beauty of the white roses. What should she do with them? Dramatically throw them in the trash can, vase and all?

Feeling like a coward, Kaleene settled for watering them, and leaving the decision until tomorrow.

The horrible squawks of a mynah bird grated across Kaleene's frayed nerves as she carried its cage back to the reception area.

"There's another one," Velma screeched, competing with the irate bird.

Wincing at the volume Velma had achieved with apparently little effort, Kaleene turned to see what she was pointing to. Sitting on the corner of Velma's desk was a tall vase filled to capacity with tulips. The petals had barely begun to open. Their color was a velvety, profound red.

Hanging from a ribbon was another very small envelope. She approached the tulips as if they might explode and tugged the card from its clasp. It went into the pocket of her lab coat, unopened. Then she whisked the tulips to her office to sit beside the white roses. They made a startling contrast, the pure white beside the intense red.

Again at closing time she went through the ritual of watering the roses, then returned with more water for the tulips. As she shrugged out of her lab coat, she transferred the card to her purse, knowing full well that she would read it the moment she was home and safely behind a locked door.

"Doc," she called softly as she tapped on his open office

door. "I wonder if you would consider loaning me your jeep some weekend soon."

"Got a yen for the big city?"

"No." She couldn't help smiling at his feisty question. "I'd like to go for a drive in the country, see some of the sights," she added to forestall any more questions.

Last night Kaleene had managed to decipher the coordinates to the land her father had owned. With a little guesswork and a lot of luck she thought she had managed to pinpoint its location on her map.

"I suppose I wouldn't mind"—he paused to scratch his bristly chin—"as long as you promise not to get lost. I kinda like having you around here."

"Great!" Her spirits lifted instantly now that she had taken another step toward reaching her goal. "When would be a good time?"

"I think this weekend. Saturday or Sunday."

"Saturday? The day after tomorrow?" she asked hopefully.

"I've been meaning to tell you that Sam Jordan—he's the farrier that was supposed to give you a ride from the bus stop—called the other day and told me he got mixed up on what day you were arriving. Said to tell you he was sorry."

Oh! Her meeting with Logan was an accident that happened simply because someone got her arrival date mixed up! Kaleene felt light-headed for a moment. But this was something she couldn't afford to think about right now. She pushed the information to the back of her mind.

"It wasn't a problem. I hope Sam's not too concerned."

"I expect he's over it." Dr. Corbin smiled indulgently

at her. "But you be sure you take one of the clinic pagers Saturday. As a matter of fact, I think you should probably carry one all the time since you're taking over more of the business these days. In the morning you get Velma to show you where we keep the extra one."

"I will."

Saturday. She set out for home at a faster pace than usual. Soon she would have another piece to the incomplete picture of the man who was her father.

"Kaleene," Fannie called the minute she stepped into the cool house. It was such a relief to be inside. The walks to work in the morning air were so calming, but the walks home in the heat of the summer evenings were nothing to enjoy. Kaleene contemplated again how long it would take to save up the down payment for a car.

"There's mail for you on the hall table." Fannie came bustling through the kitchen doorway wearing her flour-smudged apron, wiping her hands on a blue checked towel.

"Thanks, Fannie," Kaleene replied cheerfully. "How was your day?" she asked as she scooped a letter from the shallow basket on the mahogany table and followed Fannie back to the kitchen.

"Tolerable, right tolerable." Fannie returned to her task of kneading bread dough. "Been baking most of the afternoon. We'll have fresh bread with supper tonight, and plenty for breakfast tomorrow." She indicated four golden loaves cooling on racks at her elbow.

"They smell heavenly." Kaleene inhaled deeply as she leaned over the counter.

"George is taking some to my sister in the morning. He said he'd be glad to drop off that bundle of clothing for you at the Silver Spur at the same time. I spoke to Sara today. Said she was glad to loan you the jeans.''

Sara's jeans? Kaleene felt relief flush through her. She was so very glad to know they weren't Eva's.

Kaleene studied the envelope in her hand as Fannie continued talking about her day. ''Oh, it's from my dean at Purdue. . . .'' She stopped, embarrassed. ''I'm sorry! I didn't mean to interrupt you—''

''Nonsense, girl! You go ahead and open that letter now, probably do you a world of good to hear news from up north.''

''Fannie, you're a true friend.'' Kaleene leaned close and gave the woman a peck on the cheek. She perched on the edge of a chair, then hastily tore open the envelope and scanned the letter.

A pinched look formed between her eyes as she finished the short note.

''Not good news?''

''Actually, it could be. It depends on how you look at it. One thing is certain, it's flattering news.'' Kaleene nibbled at her thumbnail as she regarded the letter. ''I've been offered a teaching position, this time at Oklahoma State.''

''Are you in the market for a new job?''

Kaleene's eyes flew to Fannie's congenial features. She saw no accusatory look or judgmental attitude, just supportive interest.

''The dean tried to get me to take a teaching position at Purdue when I graduated vet school. I chose Tumbleweed instead, and I suppose he just refuses to give up.''

''But the teaching job tempts you?''

''I think it's only the shock of finding that door still open to me.'' Could that be it, she wondered? Or was she fooling herself? Her personal life had gotten so complicated since the night at the barn dance with Logan.

That thought reminded Kaleene of the note tucked in her purse. She still hadn't had a chance to read it. Maybe the best thing to do would be to toss it in the trash unopened.

There was the kitchen trash bin, right beside the back door. She could simply cross the room and toss it in. Or she could toss the dean's letter in. Or both. Maybe that would be the best action to take.

After a long soak in a hot bath, Kaleene sat on the padded stool in front of the antique vanity in her satin robe. Her damp hair fanned out on her back.

She stared down at the tiny unopened envelope. What if it wasn't from Logan? She laughed deep in her throat. Wouldn't it be a good joke on her if the tulips were from someone else?

But that was absurd. Who else other than Logan would be sending her flowers? Maybe Dr. Corbin sent them as a way of sealing their partnership.

No. That idea was absurd too. *Doc would be more apt to send a bouquet of rubber gloves*, she said to herself.

That notion started her giggling so hard her eyes watered. Dabbing at them with a tissue, Kaleene regarded the envelope again. Yes. It was time.

Clutching a damp, wadded tissue in the palm of one hand, she tore the tiny envelope open and pulled out the card.

Two more words. And his signature. She could feel the imprint his pen had made through the linen-textured card. This time it was embossed with a heart.

Kaleene stared down at it as a tear fell from her eye and dropped onto the card. It landed on the first word, then ran across to the second.

Hastily she pulled another tissue from the box and blotted the words dry. The letters looked a bit lighter, but weren't smudged. Thank goodness. Kaleene held it up for a closer inspection.

Yes, the words were still easy to read.

"Forgive me. Logan."

"A bunch of us girls are getting together and going to Amarillo this weekend. You want to come? We'd love to have you along," Velma tried to persuade Kaleene.

"No thanks. I'm planning to take a little look around the countryside this weekend. Thanks for the invitation. It was very sweet of you." Kaleene scooped up the new pager and moved to the door.

"I'll try to give you more notice next time."

Next time. Kaleene hoped there would be a next time. She thought about the dean's letter at home in her desk. Why had she saved it? Did she really believe a time would come when she would have to leave Tumbleweed?

Not before she found her father's farm. Not before she got the answers she had come looking for.

But Saturday proved differently that she had hoped. The spot she'd marked on the map was easy to find, but it turned out to be in the middle of a cattle range. There was no farmland in sight for miles, no house anywhere.

That afternoon she dropped the jeep off at Dr. Corbin's and insisted on walking home. The bookstore was on the way and she needed a new novel or two.

It was four o'clock and surprisingly cool, and the paper sack of books seemed light in her arm. As she stopped in front of the drugstore she glanced across the street at the sandwich shop. This would be a good time to have a glass of tea while she visited Mary and her mother. They had become good friends during her many lunches there.

As her foot left the curb, Kaleene caught sight of a couple emerging from the store next to the sandwich shop. The man wore a black Stetson hat, like Logan's. But on closer inspection, Kaleene saw that he was too tall, and his hair was brown, not the rich black that so mesmerized her the first day they met. It was on this very spot she realized.

That definitely wasn't Logan. But the woman . . . was Eva.

She turned her back on the couple and hastened down the street.

Their chatting and laughter followed her like a buzzing hornet.

Chapter Nine

They came Monday morning, around ten o'clock.

The waiting room was at peak capacity, the first time Kaleene had ever seen it so full. Since Dr. Corbin's summons earlier to a farm on a minor emergency, Kaleene kept herself busy caring for his appointments as well as her own.

"Doc LeGare," Velma called as she stuck her head in the exam room.

"Is it something that can't wait?" Kaleene tried to hide her harried feelings as she held on to the calico cat on the exam table.

"Another just arrived, and it's pretty big."

There was no need for her to ask what the new arrival was. Kaleene understood that Velma wasn't talking about a big patient. Her subdued tone meant flowers. "Could you put it in my office?"

"I'll try."

123

Velma's doubtful tone made Kaleene cringe. Just how big was Velma's version of pretty big?

It was late afternoon before she found out. She stood in her office stunned at Velma's newfound skill of understatement. The new flower arrangement sat on her desk and it covered the entire surface, almost brushing the ceiling. Bright pink irises, lacy dahlias, fluffy spider mums, tall spires of foxglove—Kaleene couldn't name all the flowers she was seeing.

After a bit of hunting she found the card. With no hesitation she ripped it open.

"Please. Logan."

Kaleene drew a shaky breath and stuffed the card in her purse.

The white roses and red tulips sat on the floor where Velma had placed them. Kaleene assessed their condition. The roses were a week old and no longer fresh. She threw them away and rinsed the vase before going home.

More white roses arrived the next day. But these were in a box. Kaleene saw a card taped to the outside as Velma brought the box in and laid it down without saying a word.

Kaleene angrily ripped the envelope from its tape and stuffed it in her pocket. Unceremoniously, she pulled the roses from the box and plunked them in the empty vase.

Was Logan psychic? She fumed as she filled the vase with water. How did he know that she threw out the other roses yesterday?

"This has to stop," she ranted at Velma during lunch. "He's got to stop doing this to me."

"You're right! How dare he send you flowers. The cad!"

Kaleene's mouth dropped open as she regarded Velma. Was that how her friend saw this situation?

"No, Velma, the flowers—"

"What, hon?" Velma leaned across the table and patted Kaleene's wringing hands.

Kaleene couldn't say it. They were a reminder of how devastating it was to see Logan kissing Eva at the barn dance.

Denny told her everyone expected Logan to marry her someday. He must have been toying with her, and the flowers seemed like more of the same treatment to Kaleene.

That first day here, she'd felt a deep connection with him. Even now, feeling the outline of the card in her pocket, Kaleene knew she was falling in love with him. She had known it since that day she spent at the Silver Spur Ranch at his side.

These feelings for him were too much to bear. She had to do something to get him out of her mind. The most important thing to do now was to get on with the search for information about her father. She had failed to find his farm on Saturday, and hadn't yet bothered to check the map again since that day.

"It's not just the flowers, Velma."

"I know. I realize there has to be something keeping you two apart. Do you feel up to telling me about it?"

"He and I don't view relationships in the same way. I mean, he plays the field. I . . . I can't be with someone like that."

Velma sat back and eyed Kaleene thoughtfully. "It's true Logan's always had quite a reputation. But I can honestly say he's never taken after a girl like he has you."

But what about Eva? Kaleene wanted to shout the question, wanted to cry and pound her fists on the table.

"Maybe you should give him a call, Doc LeGare," Velma suggested.

"Maybe," Kaleene halfheartedly agreed. "Velma, maybe you should stop calling me Doc LeGare." She stopped and regarded her friend's arched brows. Was she making things worse? Kaleene contemplated what Velma's vocal cords would do to her first name.

"Why don't you call me Doc L."

"Sure enough, Doc L," Velma replied, managing to stretch the letter out to two syllables. "You make that call, hear?"

"Sure enough, Velma," she replied, cheered not by the prospect of speaking to Logan but by her friend's upbeat attitude.

The card, temporarily forgotten, stayed in her pocket until the end of the day. Searching for a pen, Kaleene felt its stiffness and retreated to the privacy of her office. She scanned the little white card.

"Can I see you? Logan."

The idea of a phone call had almost become bearable, but seeing him, possibly alone? No. Still, she couldn't keep ignoring him.

This weekend she set a deadline. She'd call him on Saturday. Now she had four days to work up more courage.

Three days and three more bouquets and cards later Kaleene was helping with the charity auction for the medical center. Through a great deal of fast-talking, she'd ended up in the office, writing receipts. After this, she'd promised to go with Velma and two of her friends to the Elks lodge for

"Honky Tonk Nite." The proceeds also went to the medical center.

A short, square building on the edge of the little community was where Velma took them. Country-and-western music seeped through the edges of the door. Kaleene stuck closely to Velma and her friends as they made their way into the dark building. The smell of cigarettes filled the stale air and lent a bit of excitement to the noisy atmosphere. Colored lights strobed the ceiling and swirled sparks across the floor.

"Hey, y'all," Velma called out to different groups of people as they weaved their way through the tables to a spot near the dance floor.

"Grab that table," one of the women shouted at Kaleene, who had bumped up against the only empty one in the area. Kaleene promptly dropped into one of the chairs clustered around it and the others quickly joined her.

"Whew! We were awfully lucky," Velma declared. "Sure didn't want to have to stand by the wall. I'd never find me a man over there."

"Is that why you're here? To find a man?"

"Sure is, Doc L, and it wouldn't hurt you to do some looking either."

"Velma," Kaleene said, leaning closer so she could speak clearly over the loud music, "I think maybe you should call me Kaleene."

Velma only shrugged. "Now down to business! Are we ordering nachos or just Cokes?"

"I don't really have a preference." Kaleene had never eaten more than three bites of the cheese and chip concoction. She didn't relish the idea of sharing that information with her new friends.

The other three discussed it for a moment and finally decided to order both. "That okay with you, Kaleene?" Velma asked.

"Sure," Kaleene said, thrilled. But her delight wasn't for the food and drink. How could someone who mangled her last name so horribly pronounce her first name so sweetly?

Still, it wasn't the same as hearing it from Logan's lips.

"Now, are we making the same deal as usual?" one of the others asked.

"What's that?"

"Oh, Kaleene doesn't know about it, y'all. We shouldn't spring it on her," Velma protested.

"No, Velma." Now it was Kaleene's turn to protest. "If it's something the three of you usually do, then I'm in the deal too."

"Fair enough," the first woman said. "It's really simple. The first one who gets asked to dance pays for the drinks."

"All right," Kaleene readily agreed. She felt delighted to be a part of the group. She sat back with a satisfied grin, glanced around the room, and was suddenly looking right into Logan's face.

Her feet turned to ice as she sank into the deep blue eyes—so intensely blue, they mesmerized her.

"Hi, Logan," one of her tablemates called across the dance floor to him. Kaleene watched, paralyzed, as he rose and strode toward them. His white shirt gleamed under the sparkling lights and his bolo tie with its tiger's-eye stone stood out in bold contrast. The buckle of his belt, its hammered silver surface flashing, showed the figure of a rearing horse.

He stopped by Kaleene's chair, and she craned her head back to see his midnight blue eyes.

"Dance with me?"

He said it so low she'd almost had to read his lips. They parted slightly, showing his even, white teeth.

Go away, she fervently wished at him. But he didn't. He stood there, holding his hand out to her, hopefully, patiently.

"Go on. You still have to pay even if you turn him down," hooted one of her companions. Kaleene glanced around and caught Velma's eye. She looked panicked, unsure if she should intervene or let Kaleene handle the awkward situation herself.

"It's all right," Kaleene silently mouthed to her friend as she stood and placed her hand in Logan's. The moment her flesh touched his she knew she'd made a mistake.

Her head was spinning as Logan pulled her to the middle of the wooden dance floor. Just as he turned to face her the song ended and Kaleene tugged at the grip he had on her right hand. Logan held tight, like a desperate man gripping a lifeline, and slowly reeled her in against his solid body. She felt the bands of muscles that corded across his hard chest, rippling with each tiny movement as he adjusted his tender hold on her.

The next song began, a slow sultry country song about loving and hard times. Logan slid one hand against the small of her back and pressed her closer to him. He'd never relinquished her left hand. Now he deliberately slid each one of his fingers between hers, one at a time, until his palm sealed tightly against hers.

Logan swayed gently with her, compelling her around the dance floor with him. She felt no control over her muscles, they were his completely, his to command. Kaleene sank her head onto his shoulder, feeling the crisp, clean fabric of his shirt crinkle against her cheek.

"Kaleene." His voice rumbled deep in his chest. He spoke her name so tenderly, so full of hope.

Remembering the cards that had come with all the flowers, Kaleene thought about how he'd asked for her forgiveness, had pleaded with her to see him. She remembered the way his voice grew husky the night he dropped her off at the bed-and-breakfast. Logan had apologized for hurting her feelings, for trampling on her pride in her profession. Oh, if that was *all* that kept them apart . . .

But she would never have the conversation with him that he wanted. She couldn't bring herself to tell him she was jealous of Eva. She remembered Eva clutching at him, her fingers hooked in his shirt, then shamelessly pulling his head down, forming her hungry red lips to his.

In the darkness of the dance floor, Kaleene glanced up at Logan's lips, the same ones she had kissed less than an hour before she saw him kissing Eva. She dropped her head, anguish dimming her eyesight.

"Kaleene."

She felt the deep rumble in his chest again and pulled her head away from his shoulder. Her eyes flicked over the crowd as the song ended. Eva sat at the table Logan had risen from. Her angry, red face glared hate at Kaleene.

"Thanks for the dance," she mumbled and pulled away

from him too quickly to give him a chance to protest. She tried to shut out his voice as she fled across the dance floor but she heard him call her name, so wistfully.

"Did you know he would be here?" Kaleene rasped secretively to Velma.

"No! I had no idea. I'm so sorry."

"Oh, Velma. I didn't mean to get angry at you. It's not your fault. I'm the one who should be apologizing. Forgive me?" How strange that she should be echoing Logan's very words that he'd written on the card to her.

"Let's concentrate on having a good time." Velma patted her hand.

Kaleene sat back and tried to keep her eyes from drifting over to Logan. Several people sat at the round table with him. Some seemed to come and go, but not Eva. Logan danced with many women, but Eva only danced with Logan and a very tall, blond cowboy. The tall man's distinctive shirt with a rose embroidered across the yolk stood out in the dance-floor lights.

On the table in front of her sat her first glass of cola, only half gone. She tried to finish it but it tasted flat and bitter, just like everything else tonight. Just like Eva's face. Kaleene snickered, surprising herself with the harsh thought.

She dared a glance at Logan's table and spied Eva. Immediately Kaleene's angry bravado dissolved as Eva turned from Logan into the arms of another man. It was the tall, blond cowboy. Eva sat on his lap and began kissing him deeply, completely disregarding all the other people around her.

Kaleene was stunned! Logan sat there, less than three

feet from Eva and the man she was kissing. He acted as if it was an everyday occurrence.

Was that the kind of woman Logan had a reputation with? Kaleene suddenly felt too hot. The atmosphere grew unbearable, filled with smoke and the noise of the crowd. She stared at Eva, unable to stop watching the spectacle.

Misery filled Kaleene as she sat, temporarily alone, at the table. She needed to find Velma and get out of this place. Daring one last glance at Logan, Kaleene blanched when she saw him glaring at her.

His eyebrows drew together and a frown pulled at the corners of his mouth. He had been studying her, watching her while she watched Eva. Kaleene drew in a sharp breath, feeling her head get lighter as she did so.

Logan's scowl changed as he glanced back and forth between her and Eva. Slowly his face took on a more ominous look, a deep, foreboding look. He tapped the blond man on the shoulder, interrupting him and Eva. Logan said something to him, but Kaleene couldn't tell what it was. Could he finally be objecting to someone else kissing his girlfriend?

They rose and approached her. Kaleene sat there like a deer frozen in the headlights of an approaching truck.

''Kaleene.'' Logan's voice held some of the scowl that showed on his flushed face. ''I'd like you to meet a friend of mine.''

What should she do? Eva was the last person on earth she wanted to meet. Kaleene's eyes flicked to her glass of warm cola as she considered tossing it in his face, or better yet, in Eva's face.

"This is John Ames. We've known each other since grade school."

The man smelled faintly of alcohol and seemed a little unsteady. He must have been ordering something other than cola all evening.

"And this is his fiancée, Eva. I believe you'll remember her from the Lawford's barn dance."

Up close, Kaleene could see that the woman had the same unsteady look about her that John had.

"Yes," she almost whispered, but inside she was shouting, *Yes! The woman I saw you kissing when you should have been with me!*

"They're getting married next month," Logan continued. "Eva and I dated a long time ago, but not anymore. Although, sometimes Eva likes to feel that she can have her cake and eat it too by trying to put the moves on me like she did at the Lawfords' dance. If you'd stayed long enough you'd have seen—"

The big, blond man finally realized what Logan was saying. The silly grin slid from his face as he turned to Logan, shoving Eva out of the way.

"What're you talking about? Has Eva been making eyes at you?" His fists came up, poised in front of his brawny chest.

"Me and everybody else in the county, John. And when you're sober you know it too. So take your fiancée back to the table, so I can talk to this nice lady."

Logan turned back to Kaleene just as John took a powerful swing at him. There must have been a sound that betrayed the coming blow. Logan ducked, but not in time to avoid a glancing impact on his shoulder. Kaleene screamed as she flew out of her chair and rushed toward Logan's crumpled form. Someone pulled her away from the downed man as spectators gathered around the scene.

Logan shook his head just as John lofted a chair and swung it at him. This time he avoided the blow completely and rushed at John in a half crouch. Both men crashed to the floor, rolling over and over swinging their fists.

Kaleene felt a roaring in her ears as black dots swam before her eyes. She caught a momentary glimpse of Logan's grimacing face, blood spilling from his nose and lip as John hoisted him high and dropped him on a table. The legs of the abused table gave way with a loud crack, spilling Logan to the floor again.

John lurched forward to grab Logan and never saw the length of wood in the shorter man's hand. Logan brought it down on John's head with a dull thud and the big man toppled to the floor.

Eva tottered forward and nudged her fiancé with her toe, but he only groaned. She pointed her nose in the air and turned her back on him, making her way to another table where she plopped into the lap of another man.

Kaleene wriggled from the grasp of her unseen rescuer and knelt at Logan's side. He was battered and bleeding, and he smiled at her.

''Logan.'' Words failed her as she stared at his split lip and bruised face. His ribs must be in worse shape, she realized.

''I'm okay.'' He slurred around a lip that was already swelling. ''Honest,'' he insisted as she gave him a disbelieving look.

Another groan rumbled from the prone man beside Logan. Two men bent to help John up. "Come on, John. Time for another trip to the emergency room. We'll let 'em look at your hard head and make sure it's still just as hard as it was the last time this happened to you."

"Where do you hurt?" Kaleene asked, probing Logan's jawline with experienced touches.

"All over, Doc," he replied solemnly. "Especially here." He pointed to his mouth.

With a telling smile Kaleene leaned closer to examine his lip and felt his hand circle behind her neck. Eagerly she moved to meet him.

Logan's lips touched hers, and he savored the warmth of them for the brief moment it took him to realize that his lip really did hurt. He flinched and pulled away.

"Yes. I see," she replied in her best clinical manner. "Take two aspirins and call me in the morning."

"You can count on it." He all but growled the promise.

Chapter Ten

"At the time it never occurred to me that you weren't a willing participant in that kiss."

"And all I wanted to do was get back to you, but it was an awkward situation. She wanted a dance with me and I thought I'd only be gone a minute or two. Kaleene, I never wanted to kiss her. It happened before I knew it."

"I can see that now. I would have realized it sooner if . . ." She bit her lower lip and turned to stare into the darkness through the truck window. A few yards away the comforting glow of the lights of the bed-and-breakfast shone steadily, her refuge from the uncertainties she faced.

"If what? Please tell me. Is there anything else I can do? I'm sorry—"

"No, Logan. Please don't apologize. It was an unfortunate set of circumstances. I saw you and Eva, and Denny happened to be right there. She told me you would probably marry Eva some day."

"Denny told you that?" He reached through the darkness for her hand. "Sometimes I don't understand that girl. Denny should never have said that to you. She knows John and Eva are engaged. I never finished telling you at the Silver Spur that day—John's not only my friend, he's the foreman of Cleopatra's barn. I'll straighten Denny out about—"

"No." She held a finger up to his lips. "It happened right after she came back from seeing Clay. I remember now how upset she looked at the time. Don't you see? She must have been hurt by him."

"I see now." Logan took her hand in his and kissed the tip of her finger. "She was feeling alone and she lashed out, afraid to let you come between her and me. Apparently she could see what was happening between us better than I could. This isn't just a casual thing I feel for you."

"I know, Logan." Kaleene came into his becoming arms, sighing with contentment to be where she'd longed to be. "What I feel for you couldn't be described as a casual thing either."

"I promise you that I won't let anything like that ever come between us again, Kaleene."

"Where is he taking you this time?" Velma asked as she leaned over Kaleene's shoulder to read.

"Coyote Lake," Kaleene replied distractedly as she studied the card that had come with the yellow roses that sat on the reception area counter. "This Saturday. He says swimming and a picnic."

"Lordy. I never get to see you outside of work anymore."

Kaleene reflected on the truth of Velma's words. Since their long discussion that night after the fight with John Ames she and Logan had spent very few hours apart.

Despite his promise to forget Denny's small role in their problems, Logan had discussed it with his sister when she'd come to him with a guilty conscience after spending some time getting to know Kaleene. Logan helped Denny understand her actions and later, in private, the young girl had apologized to Kaleene.

Now they were becoming fast friends.

It surprised Kaleene that John and Logan were still good friends. Apparently John decided Eva should look elsewhere for a husband—which she wasted no time in doing—and John continued in his role of foreman as if he and Logan had had no more than a schoolyard tussle.

"Read me the card again," Velma urged her with a nudge on her shoulder.

Kaleene smiled indulgently. "These roses pale beside your beauty."

"Oh, that's so romantic." Velma sighed as she gazed off into space.

"Sounds to me like another bad case of prairie fever." Dr. Corbin's gruff voice startled the two women up off the edge of the desk.

They exchanged surprised looks and burst out into unprofessional snickering. Dr. Corbin harrumphed, spun on his heel, and marched from the reception area.

* * *

Kaleene was ready early Saturday when Logan arrived at the bed-and-breakfast. She fairly flew down the sidewalk to meet him as he stepped from the bright blue truck.

"Hi, gorgeous." His smile was wide, but suddenly grew shy as he drank in the sight of Kaleene in blue shorts and a cropped white shirt. Her long, smooth legs seemed to hold his eyes as he took the red canvas tote from her.

"Did you bring a hat?" he asked as he finally managed to tear his gaze from her and place the bag in the truck cab.

Tossing her honey-colored curls over her shoulder, Kaleene took his offered hand and climbed in. "Yes, I brought a straw hat. It's tucked in my bag with my beeper and swimsuit." Kaleene glanced down at the bag, which also held her map. She had marked a new spot on it, one she hoped would turn out to be more accurate than her last try. Somehow she'd gotten two road numbers reversed the last time she tried to locate the place where her father had lived.

"I thought we might do some sight-seeing on the way back home," she continued as he slid behind the wheel. "I checked a map and saw there are some interesting draws and creeks along the way."

"Sounds fine to me." Logan had recovered his composure now that he kept his attention focused on the road and not on Kaleene's legs.

"Terrific. How about Blackwater Draw first? And just southeast of there is a little creek I'd like to stop at." She was thrilled that the side trip had been added to their agenda without any need for explanations, which she was unwilling to give at this time.

"Sure. Part of the Silver Spur stretches up that way."

"Oh, I didn't know that." Had Logan's family been

neighbors with her father? Logan may have even known him. The thought unsettled her for some reason. To cover her unease, Kaleene began asking questions about the ranch.

They discussed Cleopatra and her filly, as well as other horses Kaleene had seen during her frequent visits to the ranch lately.

"I've decided not to breed Cleopatra anymore," Logan informed her. "I've got plenty of good broodmares from that bloodline, and there's no reason to risk any future problems with her."

"What will you do with her once her filly is weaned? A breeding ranch doesn't keep mares that don't produce, do they?"

"I'll keep her." He patted her hand reassuringly. "She's a good horse. Handy."

Kaleene scrunched her eyes in concentration.

"Easy to handle, even when you're not on her back," he explained, reading her confusion correctly. "She leads well, doesn't kick or bite."

"I see. Is she a good horse for riding?"

"Yes. If the rider has gentle hands. Cleopatra has a soft mouth and won't stand for anyone sawing on her reins. I'll keep her," he vowed.

The mild temperature spell had fled from the panhandle area several days ago and today the temperature was expected to climb high again. Kaleene and Logan planned to be in the water by that time.

Logan steered the truck to a shady spot along the six-and-a-half-mile shoreline that circled Coyote Lake.

"We could have our picnic on the tailgate of the truck,"

he suggested. We'd be higher up and have a better view of the lake.''

"That sounds nice. I love looking at this country. It's so vast." Kaleene took a moment to study Logan's strong profile. It would take a country as vast as the Texas plains to contain a man as vital as Logan. The endless sky overhead was the perfect backdrop for their picnic.

Together they spread the quilt across the tailgate and placed the picnic basket Juanita had prepared on one corner of the colorful fabric. Logan encircled Kaleene's waist with his broad hands and smoothly lifted her onto the edge.

The warmth of his hands spread up and down her sides. She instinctively gripped his sinewy arms as he lifted her effortlessly. Now she kept her hold on him, bringing her mouth to his.

Sweet, tender thoughts filled her as Logan pressed his lips to hers. The gentleness in his strong fingers, his masculine touch, sent shivers of pleasure down her spine to the tips of her toes.

It had happened. She had fallen so very deeply in love with this man, her head was spinning with passion for him. This happened every time he kissed her, she realized with sheer delight.

Out under the wide sky alone with Logan everything in the world seemed perfect. It was easy to forget all about the unanswered questions about her father. All the doubts that assailed her late at night about her decision to come to Tumbleweed were gone like so much water vapor.

Too many nights Kaleene had spent comparing this life to her former one. This place was so far from Indiana geographically and, well, sometimes it seemed like another world. The job offer from Oklahoma still sat in her desk drawer, taunting her. It would be more pay, a cosmopolitan setting, and much better hours. She would be able to afford a car almost immediately.

Logan brought his hands up to caress her cheeks, bringing her thoughts rushing back to her body. He pulled his lips from hers and gazed intently into her face. "I just want to remember you like this," he whispered.

Had he somehow read her thoughts about leaving Tumbleweed? Kaleene blanched at the idea. She didn't want to think about how Logan would feel if she left him, how it would hurt him like her mother must have been hurt all those years ago when her father left.

She kissed him lightly on the nose and turned to rummage through the picnic basket. It was time to shut out those tormenting thoughts and concentrate on the plans they'd made for today.

"Fried chicken and apple pie! Oh, Logan, you're forcing me to start that exercise routine I've been avoiding," she complained. "It seems that all I do lately is eat."

"Well, I can fix that," he proclaimed and leaned over to kiss her again.

"Oh, no you don't." She held the tips of her fingers to his ready lips. "We'll figure something else out. I really need to burn some calories before lunch."

Logan withdrew with a mock-hurt look on his handsome face. "If you don't like my plan you'll just have to come up with one of your own."

"All right. We'll go for a walk around the lake."

"Are you sure you wouldn't like to try my idea first?"

"Yes, Logan," she said scoldingly. "Now, let's get going before it gets too hot." She slid from her perch and pulled him toward the water's edge.

They walked along, content in the relative calm of the morning, accompanied by the ever-present hum of the insect life around the small lake. A lone mockingbird punctuated the stillness with high calls.

"Kaleene."

Logan startled her when he broke the silence between them. She stopped and glanced sharply at him, alerted by the serious tone of his voice.

"I've been worried about something." He moved closer and slipped his hand in hers as they moved along the trail again. "I've been wanting to talk to you about the day Cleopatra foaled, about my not telling you Beth had reported everything was fine with her."

His pace quickened slightly, just enough to betray his nervousness to Kaleene. She picked up her pace, maintaining her silence. Of the many things they'd discussed, all the time they spent together, Kaleene had never felt their relationship required any further discussion of that night. Apparently, Logan now felt it did.

"Kaleene, I think I hurt your feelings that evening."

"You think?" She arched her eyebrows at the doubt he left in his words.

"Aw, shoot. I'm such a coward." He released her hand and kicked a stone on the path. Moving away from Kaleene, Logan stepped to the edge of the water and glared out across its sparkling surface, his arms crossed on his broad chest.

Kaleene stood a few feet away, waiting for this passionate man she cared so deeply for to gain control of his feelings again.

Suddenly, Logan spun around and forced the glare from his face. "Kaleene—" He took possession of her hands in one florid movement. "I do realize I hurt your feelings that night. You were there in a professional capacity, to do a job. I appreciated it at the time. I mean, seeing you on the floor of that stall, fighting to breathe life into that little filly. The concentration and caring I saw on your face . . ." He looked up to the sky and cleared his throat before he could continue. "You were so beautiful, *are* so beautiful," he stressed. "I let my desire for you overrule my common sense.

"Please, forgive me. I swear to you right here and now"—he released one of her hands only long enough to indicate the pure, natural beauty of their surroundings—"that I will never stand in the way of your work again."

Such strong words. Such an earnest plea. And more than that. He was asking her to trust him, to take their relationship to another level, a more intense level.

Was she ready for that? She answered herself and his plea with a kiss. She pulled him closer, closer until their lips met in sweet bonding. Their shared passion, their love and desire, grew ever stronger.

Kaleene leaned back against the pickup seat, tired and happy. The water had been invigorating but it felt good to ride beside Logan and feel her muscles relax. "I'm glad you brought that float. It was fun drifting all the way across the lake." She idly studied the corded tendons in his arm as he shifted the pickup into gear and left Coyote Lake.

He laughed at some secret thought. Kaleene playfully punched his rock-hard arm. "What?" she demanded.

"Your expression," he managed to say between chuckles.

"When I first dived in the water?"

"Yes. You came up sputtering and yelling. It was such a sight." Bright reflections danced off the moisture in his eyes.

"It was so unexpected," she protested. "Who in the world would have expected to find a salt lake here in the middle of Texas?"

"We're not in the middle of Texas."

"Logan! You know what—"

"Technically," he continued to tease her, "we're up in the panhandle, and not even in the middle of that. And Coyote Lake is just one of a lot of salt lakes around here. Though I will admit most aren't as large as Coyote Lake."

"Thanks for the warning you gave me," she returned flatly.

"I couldn't help it, Kaleene. When you came out from behind the pickup wearing that tiny swimsuit my brain turned to mush. I couldn't get any words out until after you were under the water."

He was so incorrigible! She smiled, then hid it with her palm. What a strange feeling, to know the effect she had on him. Kaleene marveled at it.

"This is Silver Spur land along here." Logan pointed out her window at the lush pasture land they were passing.

His words jarred her thoughts back to the route they were driving and to the map tucked inside her bag. "That must be the way to Blackwater Draw.'' She pointed to a road they were approaching.

"Yes. Shall we stop and do a little hiking?''

"No,'' she answered slowly while tracing the route in her mind. "Let's turn left up here and see what's over this rise.''

"Okay. But you've been down this way before,'' Logan informed her as he slowed to make the turn.

"When was that?'' Kaleene tried to hide her startlement. She hadn't noticed any familiar landmarks. They passed between fields of grain, mile after mile of cultivated farmland on both sides of the road.

"Remember when I took you down to the wildlife preserve? We followed some of these roads on the way there. I took you my version of a scenic route.''

The memory of that ride came flooding back to her. They'd shared a joke about seeing the mountains and forests of the area. Kaleene watched for the crossroads that she knew must be coming soon. Maybe she should check her map. No. She was positive the crossroads would be coming into sight any minute now.

They reached the crest of a gentle rise. There it was! The farmhouse . . . and the windmill . . .

Everything looked just as it had the last time Logan brought her by this "oh so familiar'' place. This was it, this was his home. Her father had lived here.

The two-story farmhouse looked so forlorn, with its green shutters faded and drab. And the windmill—she remembered it from his letter now—stood like a lone sentry.

"It's all Silver Spur land now,'' Logan said.

"Can we stop here for a minute?''

"Why?" He looked puzzled by her request.

"I just wanted to look a bit. . . ." Her voice trailed off. She lied. She couldn't bring herself to explain why she was here, couldn't reveal the hurt she harbored over her father's abandonment so many years ago. Not even to Logan.

"Sure. We can take a look from here. But let's save our hiking for another day. It's gotten awfully hot out there."

Kaleene certainly didn't feel very hot. She felt chilled, staring at the shuttered windows of the first floor and the gloomy black patches of the tiny upper windows.

"It was a small farm," he informed her. "It was in the same family for a long time, but unworked for the last several years. Not enough land to make a profit in today's mechanized world, I suppose. I don't really know. I just heard bits of conversation about the place when my father would start to rant and rave about it."

"Why would he do that?" Kaleene's brows shot up.

"He'd wanted that land for a long time. The Silver Spur needed a fresh water source out here." Logan smiled wryly and shook his head. "My mother finally forbade him to mention the place, she was so sick of hearing about how badly he wanted it."

"Why didn't he buy it?"

"These thirty acres belonged to old Jed Pierce then. And he wasn't working it, but he refused to sell. He was as stubborn as my father. Said he'd never see Silver Spur horses on his land drinking his water as long as there was breath left in his body."

"Is that how your father got it? From Jed Pierce's inheritors?"

"No." Logan's voice grew husky for a moment. "Jed

managed to outlive my dad by a few years. Apparently Jed lost the land in a card game with a man from up north someplace. That man turned out to be as stubborn as Jed. When he died Dad bought the land from the state. No one's lived in it since. That happened in the year my parents were killed. I was twenty-two. Denny was only eight.''

The house sat on the rise, surrounded by a tangle of wild growth. Such a lonely place, she marveled. It had such a tumultuous history tied to it.

''Anyway!'' Logan cleared the air of the silence that had descended on them. ''Dad had the satisfaction of adding this little chunk of land to the map of the Silver Spur Ranch. He wanted it so badly.''

So badly. His words echoed in Kaleene's head. Logan's father, a powerful man in this area, wanted this piece of land that her father had owned. How that must have angered Logan's father. A drifter, a nobody, sitting on the land he'd wanted for so long, waited for so long.

Maybe he had felt it unjust that a drifter should end up with it. Could he have decided to take the land any way he could? All he had to do was get Kaleene's father out of his way. That was a simple thing for some men. Had Logan's father been that kind of man?

She turned to regard the profile of the handsome, powerful man beside her. How much was he like his father? Maybe that's why her father never sent for his family. Maybe he had been killed before he could send another letter asking them to come.

The glue of the envelope flap left a bitter taste on her tongue. Kaleene took a deep drink from the water glass on her rolltop desk and glanced at the clock by it. Eight-fifteen? With the envelope clutched apprehensively in her fingers she scooped up her bag and hurried down the stairs. She paused long enough to drop it in the outgoing mail tray on the entry-hall table. George would place it in the mail-box later.

As she hurried out the screen door, she glanced back at the tray one more time. The letter didn't say she would take the job, she reminded herself. She had only voiced interest, just to see what they would offer at Oklahoma State in the way of salary.

Dread followed her to the clinic, a cloud of trepidation that she hadn't been able to shake since she'd sat with Logan looking at her father's house. Since she'd found out . . . But she hadn't found out anything really. Had she? All she had right now were suspicions and fears.

Now the burning question was, how would she find out the truth?

"Hey, y'all."

Velma greeted her with all the cheer Kaleene hadn't felt in days, all the days Logan had called. But she kept giving him excuses of being too busy or too tired to see him. It was true that she was tired, bone tired—probably from the stress she felt.

"You looking forward to the long weekend?" Velma popped her gum energetically.

"I suppose so," Kaleene answered weakly, trying to hide her troubled thoughts behind a thin smile.

"Me too. Going shopping in Amarillo. You want to come?"

"No thanks, Velma. Doc's loaning me his jeep. I'm

thinking of taking a little outing to the wildlife sanctuary, maybe do a bit of bird-watching.''

''Going to do a little cooing with Logan? Maybe a few love-calls?''

Velma cackled at Kaleene's back as she disappeared down the hall. She knew Velma would chalk her reaction up to embarrassment. There would be no need to bare her soul to her friend. Not until the time came for her to leave.

Kaleene swallowed with an effort as a lump formed in her throat at the very thought of leaving the home she had found here in this tight-knit community among these open, friendly people. And the thought of leaving Logan ... Tears sprang to her eyes, and in the privacy of her office she let them fall.

Chapter Eleven

"I reckon so," Fannie called to George as he left the kitchen. She and Kaleene hurried to finish the woven pie crusts of a dozen apple pies.

"I sure hope he finds the right boxes to pack these in. I don't fancy the idea of carrying these things over to the coliseum tomorrow in baskets and whatever else we can dig up."

"Don't worry about it. I'll help you get the pies there in the morning. I'll have the use of Doc's jeep all weekend."

"That's awful sweet of you. Are you sure you'll be all right gallivanting around the countryside all by yourself?"

"I'm sure, Fannie." Kaleene picked up another strip of dough and worked it onto an apple pie. It felt so good to be here in Fannie's cozy kitchen. "Besides, I'll be back by supper. I'm helping the mayor's wife with the serving line at the barbecue. It'll be a fun celebration.''

Logan called, trying to persuade Kaleene to go to the annual celebration with him. But she had explained that it would be better if they went separately because she would be working most of the night. Thankfully, he hadn't argued too much about it—she couldn't have handled it.

''But it thrills my heart to see you and Logan getting on so.'' Fannie continued the thread of conversation she'd been on that George's brief visit interrupted.

Kaleene pulled too tightly on a strip of crust and broke it.

''That boy deserves all the happiness he can find, in my opinion. And you too,'' she declared, shaking a flour-dusted finger at Kaleene. ''I know you've had a hard time of it. It isn't easy growing up without a father. But you had a good mother. She must have taught you enough to recognize the right man when he came along. Some girls who are raised like that, they latch on to the first fella that comes along and get hitched before they're out of high school.''

''I didn't date much in high school, or in college for that matter.''

''Why do you suppose you didn't?''

''I studied too hard?'' Kaleene delivered the words like the punch line of a joke. Also, like something she now regretted.

''I'm glad to see you got a serious fella now. I'd hate to see a sweet thing like you end up at the other extreme like my little niece, Doreene. Lives down near Dallas. Won't trust a man as far as she can throw one.''

''She grew up without a father?''

"Yep. He up and left her mother with four little ones at home and one on the way. A real piece of work, that man."

"But he didn't leave because of Doreene, did he?"

"Land sakes, no! But it tore that girl up inside. Can't bring herself to let a man close. Lots of nice young men been interested, least that's what my sister tells me in her letters. That's my middle sister. Got two more you haven't met yet."

Kaleene pondered Fannie's words. Why had she asked that? About Doreene's father leaving because of her?

"Can't imagine that myself, going through life without my George."

All through school she'd thought there was no time for boys. There were too many tests to study for, too many research papers to do. There had been the rare times she had consented to go to a movie. And in college she'd met for coffee with a few of the young men who had asked.

But this feeling she had for Logan was so different. She had never cared enough about those others to let them into her heart. But Logan stole into her mind before she was aware of it. He was bold and brash, irresistible, unstoppable in his drive to take her heart—and she hadn't wanted to stop him, until now.

She was afraid of Logan leaving her. It was true. So she was going to run away from him before he got the chance to run away from her. Kaleene felt stunned at the realization.

Fannie chatted on as Kaleene let the dough strips slip through her fingers. That was why she allowed herself to get carried away with the notion that his father might have had a hand in the death of her father. This idea that she couldn't talk to Logan about her fears was an absurd attempt to avoid any chance of being abandoned by Logan.

Logan was an honorable man. Even if his father hadn't been, she could trust Logan. She could trust him with her heart and her life. He would tell her the truth, and if he didn't know all of it he would move heaven and earth to help her find it.

But was it too late? She had avoided him for days, allowing her doubts to fester like an old wound. Kaleene picked up a strip of pie crust and tugged too hard. It broke in half also. It couldn't be too late, she swore silently. Somehow she had to find the courage to tell Logan everything. Tomorrow night after the barbecue, face-to-face, she promised herself. Tomorrow night.

George did manage to locate the special boxes Fannie used to transport her homemade pies in. So it was right after breakfast the next morning when Kaleene chugged away from the bed-and-breakfast in Dr. Corbin's faded blue jeep for her drive in the country.

The map lay spread in the seat beside her, and she checked it often. Another right turn and she would be on the correct road. Kaleene noted a familiar grove of pecan trees. This was definitely the right direction.

Then she reached it, the turn to the road that led directly by the farmhouse she was searching for. She slowed the jeep and turned.

The faded wedding picture of her parents kept floating in and out of her mind. Her father's face became clearer as she spotted the house. What would it hold after all these years? Some clue as to what kind of man he had been?

Some hint as to the reason he had stayed here, never to return to his family?

Kaleene stopped the jeep at the entrance to the winding, rutted dirt drive. The house looked so forlorn. Brown balls of dead tumbleweeds hung against the wire fence that bordered the drive. She would have to steer around the larger piles of those to negotiate the drive without scratching the sides of the jeep.

Slowly Kaleene pulled the jeep from the level road onto the rutted way passing over the metal bars set in the ground that formed a guard against wandering cattle. She held her breath when she was halfway across and realized what would happen to the jeep if one of the bars suddenly gave way. It *and she* would plunge down into the shallow pit underneath.

But the bars held and the jeep thumped over the last one. A puff of breath escaped her clenched teeth. At least that was something she wouldn't have to worry about on her way out.

The ruts of the drive looked much deeper up close than they appeared from the highway. Kaleene stopped and eyed them apprehensively. Every time the powerful spring thunderstorms swept across the region the ruts would grow deeper. With the house vacant for so long the road had probably not been grated flat in years.

Sitting there just inside the gateway, Kaleene planned a path to travel on. She could stick to the left and avoid the worst erosion until she came to the sharp bend in the drive. She couldn't see beyond the pile of tumbleweeds there, so she would have to stop and reassess the trail at that point.

Kaleene let the clutch out slowly and started forward,

her hands tightly gripping the wheel. Foot by foot the jeep chugged up the road, and Kaleene stopped at the curve with a sigh of relief.

Now for the next leg of the journey. The middle looked smoothest along here, except for a short mound of the ball-shaped weeds stuck together by their clawlike branches. The whole pile was pretty short. She could drive right over them without a scratch.

Once again she let the clutch out slowly, started forward, and found herself relaxing more with each foot traveled. The front tires crunched into the tumbleweeds with ease.

Without warning, the steering wheel lurched forward, tearing itself from her grasp as her head slammed back against the seat. Then her body rocked forward just as hard.

Dazed, Kaleene pushed against the steering wheel to lever herself upright but her body felt oddly heavy. No. It was the jeep, she realized. It sat tilted forward at a crazy angle. Through the windshield the only thing she could see was the reddish brown of the drive. Had she dropped into another cattle guard?

She lifted the door handle and it swung forward out of her grasp, because of the angle, she realized belatedly. Tumbleweeds were all around the opening, obscuring her view of the ground immediately around her.

It was a strain, but Kaleene pulled her legs from the floorboard and stretched out the door for a better view. The border of weeds was narrow enough to jump. She reached back inside for her canvas tote. It held her pager, hat, and the small bottle of water George had insisted she take. Smiling at the thought of how George loved to take care of her, Kaleene leaped across the dried weeds and landed safely.

With a stick from the side of the drive, Kaleene pulled weeds away from the jeep. She groaned as she uncovered a deep rut that ran the width of the drive. It looked almost two feet deep. One of the wheels sat tilted at an odd angle. Kaleene crouched by the tire well and peered under the front. The axle was broken.

Oh, great! It would take all of her pitifully small savings to fix it, and the repair would probably take days. What a mess. Kaleene sat in the middle of the dirt drive, her head in her hands.

Well. She could sit here for the rest of the day feeling sorry for herself or go back to the road and try to flag down some help. Kaleene gathered her bag and hat and took a step back the way she had come.

Something inside her pulled her to a stop. She glanced over her shoulder at the house imposingly close. It was still early morning; she should have plenty of time for a quick look around and make it back to the paved road in time to catch a ride from someone.

The house loomed up in front of her before she realized she had fully made up her mind. Up close, she noticed the cracked, curling paint. Scrambling up the wooden steps, she peered through the grimy glass panes of the front door.

Furniture! The house hadn't been totally emptied after her father died. Kaleene tried the handle and found it locked. She had to get in somehow—she had to. All of the shutters along the lower floor were closed. But how did they lock? Examining the shutters by the door, she saw they were lashed closed with a piece of rope. The rusted metal latch hung broken and dangling from one screw.

Quickly Kaleene untied the rope and swung the shutters back. She grasped the window and pulled up. It moved so much more easily than she expected. Thrown off balance, she tumbled through the opening, landing on the dust-covered floor inside the dark room.

Climbing apprehensively to her feet, she peered through the gloom. Some light would help her search. Kaleene hurried about the room, opening the other windows and the front door. Then she took the time to survey the room she found herself in.

Faded wallpaper, its color no longer distinguishable, covered the walls of the living room and led up the staircase by the front door. A dust-coated couch, two chairs, and an odd oval table made up the sparse furniture in the living room.

There was no desk, no drawers to go through. The closet was empty, so she moved to the kitchen and discovered the cabinets all bare.

Upstairs she had no better luck. Rotting curtains hung in the dingy windows, shrouding the rooms in darkness. Kaleene pulled the dusty scraps down and opened the windows to let fresh air inside. She wandered from room to room, trying to imagine what it would have been like to have lived here with her father and mother.

The murmur of a gentle breeze filtered into the house through the open doors and windows as Kaleene sat on the top step of the dark staircase, staring down through the living room out the front door. The yard out front looked overgrown with weeds and wild prairie grasses. A few dots of bright yellow prairie zinnias gleamed like neon in the high noon sun. A sob escaped her trembling lips, surprising her. This place was affecting her more than she cared to admit.

Kaleene pulled a tissue from her bag and wiped her dusty face. She tilted her head back and swabbed at her neck, managing to get most of the grit off. A flicker of light caught her eye; sunlight from one of the upstairs windows bounced off a picture hung above her.

She jumped to her feet and touched it to see if it was real. The gloom must have hidden the picture from sight when she first climbed the stairs. So many years of dust covered the glass that Kaleene couldn't make out the image.

The frame weighed heavy in her hands as she removed it from its peg and carried it down out into the light. Sitting on the porch steps, she pulled tissues from her bag and scrubbed at the glass. A face came into view. It was a woman, a very young woman. As recognition dawned on her she almost dropped the glass. It was her mother!

A heart-stopping pang flashed across her chest. Her father had taken this with him that day so long ago when he deserted his family. Tears tracked down her face and dripped onto the portrait. The tissue disintegrated as she scrubbed at the wet splashes. Kaleene wrapped her arms around the portrait, hugging the thick frame to her chest as sobs shook her bowed shoulders.

Cicadas and grasshoppers sang from the bushes and weeds around the dilapidated farmhouse. Hot air rose in wavering patches as the sun inched toward the west. Kaleene held the picture in a tight embrace and grieved for her loss.

The quiet rasp of insect noise surrounded her. Suddenly a high-pitched beeping noise shattered the air. Kaleene jumped up and flew to the doorway before she realized what it was. The pager in her bag had been activated. The effect couldn't have been more devastating on her nerves than if the porch roof had caved in above her.

She lurched to the bag on the step and pulled out the offending device, pressing the silver bar to silence it. Velma or Dr. Corbin would be expecting her to call the clinic soon. But the nearest phone had to be miles away, she realized as she scanned the flat horizon. The best thing to do would be to return to the road and try to flag down a ride.

After a long drink of water, she paced quickly down the drive. The sun beat unbearably on her neck. Without stopping she pulled her hat from the tote and felt instant relief. Now she could make it. She hurried along, the heavy picture bumping against her side as she jumped over the deep rut Dr. Corbin's jeep was stranded in.

No cars or trucks were anywhere in sight down the long ribbon of black the road cut in the flat landscape. Resolutely she started north toward Tumbleweed, hoping that the first vehicle to top the rise wouldn't be Logan's.

Minutes, then an hour dragged by and still no cars came. She thought back to the two times she had ridden down this road with Logan. Had they met any traffic? She couldn't remember.

Hours passed before she reached the first turn. Kaleene sat by the road and sipped the last of the water from

George's bottle. It was empty now, despite her determination to take small swallows once she saw how deserted the road was. Still, she shouldn't get dehydrated before she reached a major highway. Why didn't someone come?

Maybe it would be best to cut across the fields and try to get to the town on her own. She rummaged through the bag for the map, then remembered it was still in the jeep. Kaleene smacked her palm against her forehead. She had walked right by it leaving the house.

There was no other choice but to stick to the roads. At least the route was fresh in her mind. Now she didn't care if Logan was the first person to find her. Kaleene chuckled as she rose and continued her walk down the narrow road.

"Logan will find me out in this heat, carrying a darn heavy picture and laughing to myself." She spoke to the air that shimmered about her. "He'll think I've suffered a heatstroke, or need to be locked up." The real danger of that sobered her thoughts and she wiped her forehead. "Yes. I'm still sweating. No danger of heatstroke right now." She laughed at herself again and wiped drops from her eyes.

A rattle, a brittle, cracking noise cut off her laughter, freezing it in her parched throat. Kaleene whipped her hand away from her eyes. In the road, no more than an arm's length away, coiled a rattlesnake, its scales glistening in the sunlight. Tiny eyes regarded her, threatening, daring her to move.

Her muscles clenched, hard. The hot air solidified in her lungs. The snake would strike, her nerves screamed. If she moved it would strike, maybe down low on an ankle, or up high. Her mouth was totally dry.

Coldly, calculatingly, Kaleene weighed her odds of backing away, of coming out of this encounter unscathed. She came up with nil. If the snake struck down low she could possibly survive, could get the poison out. Maybe she could reach the town before—

The thought froze in her mind as the sleek creature slithered a foot to her left. She rolled her wide eyes in that direction. Nothing there. Where was the snake going? What does it matter, she berated herself.

Gingerly she shifted her weight to her left foot and slid her right one away from the snake. The tail lifted and shook for a moment. Kaleene's muscles locked.

A second later she thought her ears were playing tricks on her. The rasping sound was echoed behind her. Then it came again. Another rattler!

Logan, please! Her silent plea filled the vast, open landscape.

The mirage formed in the corner of her eye, a shimmering object wavering in the heat rising from the pavement. The distant roar of a pickup buzzed at the edge of her awareness, then filled her head driving out the wicked sounds of the snakes.

How she wished the mirage were true. The image of the truck solidified, bright blue and glinting chrome. Her eyes locked on it as it approached down the shallow rise, slowing as the driver leaned forward to peer through the windshield. He slipped the pickup's engine into neutral, allowing it to roll to a stop at the bottom of the rise.

Kaleene wanted to wipe her eyes to see if the image would vanish. Was it real?

Her heart leaped into her throat as the snake behind her

slithered forward into the right edge of her vision. She stood between the twin lines of peril now. The one in the middle of the road, a diamondback, she clinically noted, slithered to her right. Kaleene stifled an urge to laugh at the absurdity of her noting the snake's classification. This wasn't exactly the time for field observations.

The snakes were moving together in front of her.

In the distance, the pickup door opened slowly and a man's head and shoulders appeared. He stood on the chrome running board, pointing at her. Did he want her to do something? Was he crazy? Didn't he see the snakes right in front of her?

A deafening boom split the heat-shimmering air, rocking Kaleene back onto the ground. The moment her elbow touched the hot asphalt another volley echoed through her ringing ears. She felt tiny pinpricks on her legs.

She lay there, clutching her mother's portrait to her chest, unable to move. Logan's face swam into view before her burning eyes. His face was flushed and angry, she thought. Why?

Little white clouds wavered over his head. They bounced around. No. He bounced around. She rolled her head to the side. He was carrying her to his pickup.

"The snakes—"

"Shh, they're dead. Everything's all right." He hugged her closer and kissed her forehead.

"But I felt . . . One of them bit me on the leg." She tried to make him understand.

"No it didn't." He placed her in the blessed coolness of the pickup. "I shot you."

"What? You shot—"

Logan's mouth claimed hers. He ran his hands searchingly through her hair. He crushed her body to his. He took her breath away.

"Kaleene," he murmured around his ardent kisses. "Kaleene." It was a fervent prayer.

Chapter Twelve

With an effort Kaleene opened her burning eyes only a thin sliver as Logan lifted her from the pickup. "Where are we?" She laid her head on his shoulder and encircled his neck with her arms, feeling the strength in his arms as he carried her up wide steps.

"Home," he replied tersely.

"Home? But you shot me. I should be in a hospital," she protested.

"You shot her?" Kaleene recognized Sara's alarmed voice. Denny's face came into focus briefly as she hopped along beside her brother.

"Want me to call an ambulance, Logan? Or the sheriff? Is he going to arrest you?" The young teen poured questions out in a rush.

"Hush, Denny," Logan scolded. "Nobody's going to be

arrested. Sara, help me get her on the couch in the living room.''

"Oh, blood!" Denny squealed at the sight of the red stain on the sleeve of Logan's shirt. "Her leg!" She pointed as she found the source of the blood.

Logan must have cut her pant leg away. Kaleene had no idea when. She closed her aching eyes as Logan laid her down and knelt her at her side.

Sara planted a hand firmly on Denny's shoulder. "Denny, go to the kitchen and get a pitcher of water and a tall glass."

Kaleene realized Denny had left when Sara continued. "Now tell me what happened."

"Velma called me. Kaleene didn't answer a page, and Doc got worried. He thought she was at the wildlife preserve. I didn't find her there, so I followed a hunch and went looking elsewhere." He paused and took a steadying breath. "Thank God I did."

Logan's voice brushed over Kaleene like a velvet blanket, soothing and comforting. She felt her head growing heavy again, and her ears seemed to be filling with cotton.

"Here's the stuff," Denny proclaimed loudly in her excitement as she returned with Juanita in tow. "Is she still alive?"

"Denny!" Logan shouted this time.

"Honey, she'll be fine," Sara assured her.

Juanita assessed the situation and calmly instructed the excited girl. "I'll get the first-aid kit, Denny. You go to the kitchen and boil water. Fill every pan you can find and stay there to watch them."

"Good idea," he told the housekeeper as Denny dashed from the room.

Someone laid a wet cloth across Kaleene's forehead and puffy eyes. It felt wonderful, so cool. Kaleene wanted to thank them, but the effort to form the words was just too much for her right now.

"Apparently she had walked a long way in the heat. Too far. Somehow she stumbled on a couple of diamond-backs."

Sara's sharp breath hissed between her clenched teeth.

"I pulled my rifle from under the seat and shot them. The second bullet shattered on the pavement when it passed through the snake, and a couple of fragments ricocheted and scratched Kaleene's leg. Scared the life out of me."

"I wasn't bitten?" Kaleene murmured. Of course she wasn't. Logan had told her that already.

"No, honey." Logan kissed her flushed cheek. "You weren't bitten. You just got a couple of scratches and way too much sun. That's all."

"And you shot me," she reminded him in a dreamy voice.

"And I'd do it again," he reassured her.

"Boss!" An excited voice accompanied the banging of doors. "Denny said you—" The voice was drowned out as the noise of other people entered Kaleene's conscious-ness. The babbling began to fade in and out as someone held a glass to her lips. Water trickled into her parched throat.

The portrait. What had happened to her mother's por-trait? Kaleene tried to struggle upright and force the glass away. She wanted to ask Logan if he had seen a portrait in the road when he found her. She tried to call to him but couldn't tell if he heard her. The voices around them were so loud. Then they faded away as she drifted down into soft grayness.

His room, that's where she was. The dark masculine colors of Logan's bedroom were all around her. Sunlight filtered in through the parted draperies of the two long windows nearby. Kaleene rolled her head away from the soft light and gazed around the expansive room. Piled in one chair were a pair of Logan's jeans. A shirt lay nearby.

He must have carried her up here earlier this afternoon. She rolled her head back to the windows that were open to a view of the entry drive. No, she frowned in confusion. Those windows were on the front of the house, and it faced west. The sun wasn't shining on them; that's what was bothering her. It must be morning. She'd slept through the afternoon and night!

Kaleene rubbed her eyes and propped herself up on one elbow. She pulled the light covers back and felt a twinge on her left leg. More cautiously she sat up and pulled her leg from under the sheet. Two small bandages were taped low on her shin. She probed the area gently, wincing at the slight sting she felt.

Leaning back against the deep pillows, Kaleene yawned and stretched her rested muscles. Her feet still felt sore from the long walk, but other than that she felt completely recovered from the ordeal. Her tangled mass of honey-colored hair spilled over her shoulder as she moved to the edge of the bed.

What she needed now was a long, hot shower. It would

be sheer heaven. Then, if she could locate some clean clothes, she could be off to hunt up something to eat.

But where were her clothes? Kaleene looked down at the pink nightgown she wore. It was one of her own! Fannie must have gotten it to her somehow.

She stretched one more time and that's when her eyes alighted on it—the portrait of her mother. Someone had placed it on the bedside table, propping it against a brass lamp.

Her hand darted out to touch it, to confirm that it was real. It was. She hadn't dreamed it all. Kaleene picked up the heavy frame, unconsciously polishing the glass. She'd never seen a copy of this portrait before. It must have been her father's favorite.

Carrying it over to the brighter light of the window, Kaleene studied the youthful face. She looked just like she did in the wedding picture Kaleene treasured, so young and full of life with no sign of the sadness that would later haunt her eyes after her husband deserted her. Why had he done it? Kaleene wondered again.

She scrubbed at the glass with the heel of her hand. It still seemed cloudy. It would be best to take the glass out and clean both sides.

The plush carpet scrunched luxuriously between her toes as she stood in Logan's bathroom and pried the back panel out of the frame. It was hard work trying not to damage the precious object, but the panel finally loosened enough to be pulled free.

A piece of yellowed paper lay across the back of the portrait, probably to protect it from the wooden panel, she surmised. She lifted it by a creased corner and laid it on the marble vanity. The other side was covered with writing. Kaleene stared at it for a moment, unable to decipher what she was seeing.

Gathering up the picture, frame, and paper, Kaleene hurried back to the lamp by Logan's bed. She spread the pieces out on the thick coverlet and turned on the lamp. The bright light washed across the yellowed surface of the paper. It was a letter, she realized, a letter from her father.

My Darling Wife,

I can't ask you to forgive me, I can't forgive myself. I wanted so desperately to keep the beautiful life we had together, but it wasn't to be. I couldn't be there for you when you needed me. I left that day only intending to look for work, but when the time came to return home and disappoint you once again I couldn't bear to do it.

I've made a good start here in Texas. Due to the luck of the draw in a poker game I've come into some land. It could be a good home for our small family. I will send for you and our precious child when I have earned enough money for bus fare. I can only ask you to please understand, forgiveness doesn't seem attainable to me.

Your Loving Husband

It was wrong, all wrong. He'd taken the big portrait with him that day when he left. He must have planned to leave them. Was he such a weak man that he had to lie in a letter he never even mailed? Kaleene glanced at the date on top of the letter.

Ten years! It was written ten years before the letter he had found the courage to send them. Kaleene laughed bitterly. He had lived and worked here for ten years, secure in that house while she and her mother scrimped and saved just to have enough to eat.

What a blind fool she had been, to worry about whether he left because of her, whether the added pressure of a child was what drove him away. But that hadn't been the reason. He had been weak in spirit and conscience. Somehow that thought struck a familiar memory, something her mother had once said about him when Kaleene had asked one of her endless questions.

Her mother commented that he wasn't a strong man. At the time Kaleene thought she meant he wasn't physically strong. But now, remembering her mother's tone of voice, she knew her mother meant a different kind of weakness. It was something her mother must have forgiven in him long ago. She had held no bitterness in her heart for him, just forgiveness.

Kaleene put down the letter and picked up the portrait. Such a remarkable woman. Could she bring herself to do the same? Could she forgive her father now that she knew the whole truth behind his desertion of his family? She could try.

"Oh, Mother," Kaleene cried. Silent sobs racked her body as she stared into the unmoving face.

She didn't hear the bedroom door open, nor see Logan's worried expression as he peered inside. A huge bouquet of flowers, almost as broad as his shoulders, was clutched in one hand. As he registered Kaleene's distressed posture he dropped the flowers and swept in the room.

"Kaleene, where are you hurting?" His tone was edged with a sharpness of alarm, but low, almost an urgent murmur. He knelt in front of her, his eyes roaming over her silently quaking body.

"Logan." Kaleene laid the portrait on the table and threw her arms around his neck, burying her wet face against his shoulder.

"Are you hurt? A doctor from the medical center was out here and checked you over. He said after a little fluids and rest you'd be fine. But if there's something he missed—"

She hiccuped, then tried again. "No, I'm fine." She released her iron grip on him and sat back, wiping her eyes. "All I needed was a good night's rest."

Logan took a corner of the bedsheet and dabbed at her cheeks. His touch was so tender. She leaned into it.

"Two nights' rest," he corrected her. And a long day in between."

Her eyes flew open. "You're not kidding? I've been asleep for two days?"

"Yes, and you're going to stay right where you are for a while. I'll get a doctor out here to check you over."

"But—"

"One who's used to treating patients with fewer than four legs," he interrupted her.

She sank back against his soft pillows. Logan took the opportunity to fuss over her, fluffing the pillows and adding to their considerable height by bringing more from the couch.

"I can't believe I've been out that long."

"Well you have, sleeping beauty. The doctor said it was

normal after the experience you went through. He had you on an IV the first twenty-four hours with a nurse here to watch you.'' Logan returned to the table by the bedroom door and poured a generous glass of ice water from an insulated pitcher.

Kaleene checked her hands. A circular Band-Aid covered a tiny spot on the back of her left one. Logan returned and saw her examining the covering.

''And if you don't want to be stuck again, I suggest you drink all the water you possibly can before the doctor gets here.''

''Honestly, there's no need to call him, Logan.'' She took the glass and drank deeply. Her throat didn't feel in the least bit parched, but she drank to humor Logan; he looked so worried. As she handed the empty glass back he beamed an approving smile at her.

''I missed the mayor's benefit barbecue!'' Kaleene started to rise again only to be pushed gently back on the pillows. ''But Fannie and George, they must have been so worried—''

''Not anymore. They were out here last night to see for themselves that you were all right.'' He let his hands drop away from her shoulders, satisfied that this time she would stay put.

''Oh. Did they bring my gown then?''

''Yes.'' Logan settled on the edge of the bed. ''Who is she?'' He inclined his head at the portrait resting on the bedside table. At Kaleene's silent, wide-eyed glance he continued. ''Fannie saw it on the table there and took an awfully intent look at it. I questioned her about it but she just told me to ask you. You had it clutched so tightly I practically had to pry it out of your hands when I put you in the truck.''

Kaleene steeled herself for a stunned reaction, then answered, ''My mother.''

Logan arched a brow. That was so much less than she expected.

''How did you come to have it with you when you were out joyriding in Doc's jeep?''

The jeep! She had completely forgotten about it! ''Oh, Logan! I left Doc's—''

''The jeep is in the repair shop. It'll be back in commission by midweek.''

''He must be furious with me.''

Logan glared at her. ''You've got to be kidding. He's just thankful to have you still here in one piece. You don't know how much that man has come to rely on you, Kaleene.''

Guilt flooded through her. Only a few short days ago she had toyed with the idea of leaving Tumbleweed. And all because she couldn't face the idea of how serious her relationship with Logan was becoming. The idea she'd dreamed up that Logan's father would cause a man's death just to gain land . . . It was her own form of running away. She had her weaknesses too, she realized.

Logan reached out to touch her frowning face. ''Don't worry about Doc being on foot either.''

''On foot? You mean, without his jeep. I hope he doesn't try walking to and from work. Not while we're having this hot spell.''

''I thought I just told you not to worry about that. His jeep broke down on Silver Spur land, on a road I should have had blocked off. We take care of our obligations here. The ranch bought a Bronco for the clinic. He said you'd be stuck with his old Willis when you and it are both back in commission.''

"The ranch? Don't you mean you bought him a Bronco?''

"There you go again, trying to change the subject. Now, tell me what you were doing taking this portrait of your mother out there with you.''

"I didn't have it with me when I left Tumbleweed.'' Now Kaleene got the stunned reaction from Logan that she had expected earlier. This would be hard, but she felt determined to set things straight between them. Logan deserved to know the truth—of her past, her reason for coming to Tumbleweed.

"Please, let me start at the beginning. LeGare isn't the name I was born with.''

"But—''

She held up a hand to forestall his questions. "Let me explain it to you. It's a bit of a complicated story.''

His face grew somber as she recounted her early life, how she and her mother had struggled after her father left. She touched lightly on the sorrow of her mother's death months before her graduation from veterinary school.

"But the reason I came here, why I ended up in Tumbleweed, was to search for clues as to what kind of man my father was. The postmark on the one letter we ever received from him was Tumbleweed, Texas. I found records of him owning a farm at the courthouse here. So I went looking for that farm. I found my mother's portrait there.''

"What was his name?" Logan sounded deeply troubled. His brow furrowed as he waited for her answer.

"Randall Wells. He's the one who got the farm from Jed Pierce, the farm your father wanted so badly."

"And you didn't tell me? Why, Kaleene?"

"I couldn't. I couldn't tell anyone. I wanted to find out what I could about him, but I didn't want to hear other people's opinions of him, especially if they knew they were speaking to his daughter. I just wanted to find out on my own. Can you understand? So I could have some control of what I learned, of how much I learned."

"I see." He kept his gaze locked on her solemn brown eyes. "But Kaleene—"

"I know. It doesn't explain my nutty behavior these past few days." She shifted nervously under his scrutinizing gaze. "After I found out your father had wanted that piece of land so badly, I though he might have done something, maybe had a hand in my father's death."

Logan's face drained of color. "How could you think . . ." His voice, hoarse with strain, faltered.

"I'm so sorry." She captured his limp hands, clutching them to her. "It was a stupid notion, one I formed out of thin air. I realize now that I was just grabbing at straws, trying to justify to myself why my father never sent for us. It was based on a silly little girl's fantasy about a mythical father she wanted to love her."

"Oh, Kaleene." Logan breathed her name, turning his hands in hers to return the grip she had kept.

"Don't you see? If he was murdered before he could send for us . . . I realize how absurd my reasoning seems now." Her eyes dropped from his face; she felt unable to bear the intensity of his gaze. "I invented that fantasy to cover up for my own fear. I was afraid of becoming too involved with you, of leaving myself vulnerable to you. Someday you might leave me too. . . ."

She shifted nervously and forced herself to meet his eyes again. "Please forgive me. I know the truth now, the truth about why he never sent for us. It was in the back of the picture." She indicated the yellowed paper lying on the table. "He wasn't strong enough to handle the pressures of supporting a family, of having other people rely on him."

"You learned this from his letter?"

"Mother tried to explain it when I was younger, but I didn't understand it. No young girl wants to think of her father as anything but perfect." Kaleene's face reflected the inner pain she felt at voicing her thoughts. "He wrote that he planned to send for us, but he was here ten years at least, and never did. That's the reality of the situation."

"I remember when he died, Kaleene. I remember my father talking about it with Clayton Lawford. Your father was working for Clayton on one of his oil rigs. There was some kind of accident involving machinery at the drill site."

She closed her eyes and nodded her head. "I see. I'm glad to know. I can put it behind me now."

"But Kaleene, was there another reason you've been so distant with me lately?"

"You were aware of it?" she asked with surprise. "I didn't want you to feel that way. I was having trouble handling the fact that I was falling so deeply in love with you."

"You were?" he asked as his face broke into a wide grin. "I mean, you are?"

"Now wait, Logan. I need to explain. I had this irrational fear of you abandoning me if I fell in love with you. Do you understand? That's why I acted so silly about Eva."

"Now you know how foolish that was," he admonished her, and softened his words by kissing her cheek. "I could never be interested in any other woman when I'm so deeply in love with you."

"In love with me? Logan—"

His mouth claimed hers, just as his heart had claimed her without her realizing it. The moistness of his kisses left a burning trail down her jaw, just as they had the night of the barn dance. But this time there would be no pulling back. This time she was free to revel in the feel of his arms around her, the strength in his body as he held her tight. She was free to tell him.

"Logan, I love you, I love you." Her words were breathy, barely more than a sigh amid the fervor of his kisses, but he heard them clearly.

"Kaleene," he murmured her name so sweetly, "I love you. I'll never be without you again."

Yes. He was right. This is how they would be for the rest of their lives. Together. Nothing could come between them because their love was stronger than anything else in the world.

"We'll be married here at the ranch," he said, then kissed her palms one at a time.

"Oh?" she teased. "I don't recall being asked." Perhaps not verbally, but his kisses and caresses had spoken to her heart, had made promises of unyielding love.

Logan pulled himself from her arms only to lunge down and sweep her up effortlessly. She recovered her breath as he carried her across the hardwood floor and settled her gently on the velvety soft couch.

Very seriously, Logan knelt on one knee, his eyes sober. His jet black hair was tousled from her caresses, and Kaleene reached out to rake her fingers through its mesmerizing strands.

Logan captured her hand halfway to its goal and pressed her still-sensitive palm over his heart. "Kaleene LeGare," he said, his tone so formal, his gaze so unwavering, "will you consent to be my wife?"

No muscle twitched, no finger moved as he held himself poised for her to answer.

Her heart leaped to respond to his question and the rest of her body rushed along behind it. "Yes. I will be your wife."

He crushed her to his chest, murmuring her name over and over into the soft curls of her long hair. A single tear of joy traced its way down her flushed cheek. She had found what she didn't even know she had been looking for.

"We're going to share a dorm room when we go to college," Denny explained to Kaleene as the two tacked up their horses side by side in the middle stable of the Silver Spur. "She's been my best friend since seventh grade and she's always planned to go to A & M too."

"Oh, Denny, that will be wonderful for you." Kaleene settled the heavy saddle on Cleopatra's back.

Denny's dalmatian danced around their legs, getting in the way, but managing very nicely to avoid being stepped on. The puppy had been a present from Kaleene, a payment from one of her grateful clients. Now the dog had grown so big, he could barely be called a puppy any longer.

They led their horses into the clear, crisp autumn air. Denny swiftly mounted her Leopard Appaloosa and Kaleene followed suit, mounting Cleopatra a little less gracefully. She sat atop the mare, Logan's wedding present to her, marveling at the beauty of the quarter horse. Though the ceremony wouldn't take place until this weekend, Cleopatra was officially hers, papers and all.

Every spare moment of Kaleene's time had been spent here at the ranch since that wonderful day Logan asked her to marry him, and now she felt completely a part of the place. He'd told her that was his motive for the early wedding present.

"Is Logan really going to make you train Cleopatra's filly?" Denny asked skeptically as she lightly prodded her horse.

"Yes. I believe he is. But with a great deal of help from him, I'm sure." Kaleene had no trouble guiding Cleopatra along beside Denny and her horse.

"Well, if he doesn't help, you just ask Jess. He knows what he's doing," Denny declared. "But honestly, Kaleene, I can't imagine Logan missing an opportunity to spend any amount of time with you. Sara says he's love-struck in the worst way. She means he's deeply in love with you," Denny hastened to explain.

"I suppose that's better than saying he has prairie fever," Kaleene said to chide the teenager.

"Huh?"

"Just something Doc said." Kaleene's eyes twinkled.

"Oh. I see," Denny humored her. A companionable silence settled between them as they wound their way up a small rise. Denny twisted around in her saddle, peering back at the ranch spread out below them. Its buildings created a tidy pattern amid the green pastures and paddocks dotted with horses. "I swear!" She shook her head in disgust.

Kaleene looked with alarm at Denny's screwed-up features.

"He has a sixth sense when it comes to finding you," Denny complained, answering Kaleene's questioning look. She pointed to the ranch and Kaleene followed her outstretched arm.

Logan was cantering a big bay up the rise toward them.

"Honestly! Can't he give us just a few minutes to talk?"

The horse he rode champed at the bit, but Logan maintained his control of the snorting beast. A black Stetson hat was planted firmly on Logan's head. A plaid shirt, its pearl snaps glinting in the sunlight, stretched across his muscular chest.

"I'm going to the creek!" Denny announced. "I'm so sick of all this love-struck stuff," she swore as she galloped away on her spotted horse, her spotted dog trailing close behind. Kaleene hadn't managed to find a spotted outfit yet but she hadn't given up.

Logan cantered the horse closer, its mane and tail flying out with each hard stride. Well-worn leather chaps covered his sinewy legs. She could see the dimples in his cheeks, deepened just now by his determined grin. Those dimples were probably what first attracted her to him.

No, she corrected herself as he pulled the stamping horse to a jarring stop beside her, it had been his midnight blue eyes. She remembered clearly now that she was staring into them. They had seemed hooded, like a bird of prey. And she was the prey, she knew as he reached over and pulled her from her saddle. He held her in his lap.

He had captured her, she was his. Her arms encircled his neck as their lips met. And he was hers.